CLASS OF '62

by
PETE LIEBENGOOD

CHAPTER 1

The air conditioning was on the fritz again. Orrin Burdette, as conscientious a chief engineer as you can find for twenty grand a year, could feel the control room temperature rise by the minute. He was perspiring at the temples and his brand new seersucker shirt was gushing sweat under his arms. He'd complained about the problem to management too many times to mention. "Cool those tape machines and film chains or they'll burn out." Didn't accomplish anything.

Orrin briefly considered making an issue of it again by picking up the hot phone to the station owner, but decided there was no use getting riled up and having his blood pressure spike again. And, it was common knowledge among employees that station owner Edna Pendleton Wright disdained complainers as ungrateful. Besides, the Dodgers had a rally going. Maury Wills, who was sitting on fifty-two stolen bases for less than half a season, was on first with Willie Davis and the heart of the L.A. batting order coming up. Orrin cupped his Zenith transistor radio to his ear

— a Royal 500-H, the only commercial model suitable for a broadcast engineer. Somehow he managed to keep tabs on both the Dodgers' game and the ABC feed of *Lawrence Welk's Dodge Dance Party* playing on several monitors surrounding him. "At the moment, however, Dodger announcer Jerry Doggett held the majority of Orrin's attention. "Wills has a sizeable lead as Miller works from the stretch. Here's the two-one offering. Wills is off... the ball is high and... Maury beats the throw down to Schoendienst."

"Yes! Number fifty-three," Orrin shouted, rising out of the chair from which he baby-sat KEYT-TV's master control. "Way to go, Maury!" Orrin was the rare engineer who'd prefer reading about baseball in the *Sporting News* over anything in *Popular Mechanics*. Oddly enough he never played baseball at any level. He only got interested in the sport when the only girl he ever dated had an uncle who had a cup of coffee in the major leagues as a utility infielder for the Cincinnati Reds.

At age 65, Orrin's job was his life. He'd never married and had no family. At most TV stations the chief engineer is usually the "big dog," the overseer. Orrin, however, always downplayed his status among his fellow engineers. He liked to get his hands dirty. He didn't mind working board shifts on weekends so that the other engineers who had families could have the time off. He was good at his job and not above occasionally bragging about his technical skills.

Unfortunately, there was no one in the building for Orrin to share the joy of Wills' stolen base. The station's news anchor, Bill Hurley, always the last to leave, had exited the building more than two hours ago.

"...Wunnerful! Wunnerful! That was the lovely Champagne Lady, Norma Zimmer, ladies and gentlemen, with Jimmie Roberts along side singing a peppy medley from the Broadway musical South Pacific…"

Orrin glanced up at the large circular master control clock. Welk's show was due for a commercial break in one minute. Time to tend to business and put his radio aside even though Wills was a threat to steal third. He got up out of his chair. At 6' 3" and rail thin, Orrin looked like a Slinky in reverse as he struggled to stand erect. After another check of the clock, he picked up the weighty commercial program log and studied it. It's a board operator's Bible. The log details exactly what commercials air and when — down to the second. The book was bound in leather and tethered to the console by a sturdy chain. Orrin double-checked his film chains: Brown's Pharmacy was in A, Trenwith's Department Store in B.

As he placed the logbook back on the counter top and retrieved his radio, a loud banging on the delivery door at the rear of master control startled Orrin. It puzzled him because no one ever came to the door at night — not in the eight years he'd been working there.

"… and, Wills goes…Oliver's throw is high…not in time. Number fifty-four…"

The excitement of Jerry Doggett's radio call made Orrin forget about the door, if only for a second. He tried his best to imagine the play — Wills kicking up a cloud of dirt as his lead foot slapped against the third base bag. Another round of heavy banging snapped Orin out of his trance. He was pretty sure it was louder than before.

"Who's there?" Orrin hollered, knowing his voice probably couldn't penetrate the heavy metal door.

No response; just more banging.

Orrin looked back at the clock. On the job it was his master. He paused to recognize he was fully engaged in yet another episode of beat the clock. Thirty seconds to break. The Lennon Sisters were scheduled to perform next. God forbid he should fail to come out of the break clean. Dang! Nothing had happened on his shift for months, suddenly he's in the middle of a three-ring circus: Wills, Welk and whoever was at the door. Without hesitating, Orrin moved to the door and hurriedly pushed down on the metal bar to open it. He didn't look to see who it was, didn't have time. He just turned and scurried as best he could for the controls. Ten seconds to spare. He glanced up at the big, black encased TV that monitored what was on KEYT's air. It was perched like an eagle on a shelf above him. He was shocked by what he saw. There were two images: a smiling Myron Floren on the accordion and the reflection of a hooded intruder carrying what looked like a baseball bat and moving quickly toward him. The distorted image of the faceless figure caused Orrin's entire body to clutch. He sensed his chest tighten like it was in a vice. How could this be happening to him with only four months to go before retirement? He'd already coughed up the down payment on a trailer in a park in Phoenix. So often he'd imagined spending his days on his ham radio; "This is K8 Sugar Dog Easy. Anyone out there?"

The picture in the air monitor suddenly disappeared leaving the screen black. Instinctively, Orrin reached for the flashing yellow button and punched up film chain A. He tried taking a deep breath. It failed to unlock his chest. The countdown leader flashed in the preview monitor. Three, two, one...

"… If confidence and reliability are what you're looking for in a pharmacist, look no further than Brown's Pharmacy, 1600 State St. For over thirty years…"

Orrin dropped to his knees on the hard control room floor and clutched at his chest. Was this the heart attack his doctor had repeatedly warned him about if he didn't stop smoking? Perspiration suddenly ran laps across his forehead. Orrin sensed someone now standing over him but could do nothing about it. As his window of consciousness began to close he was left to wonder what would happen to him next. In a million years he wouldn't have expected it to be the sound of the air conditioner kicking back on.

CHAPTER 2

Edna Pendleton Wright poured her guest, the Honorable Judge Winston A. Garland, a requested liberal splash of Drambuie. They'd just finished a candlelight dinner of Peking duck served with Chinese pancake, scallions and plum sauce – Edna's chef's specialty.

The judge had taken it upon himself to sit on the same side of the long Maplewood dining table as Edna. It was the first time he'd done that. Clearly he was interested in more than just the spectacular sights of Santa Barbara at night afforded by the large picture windows in Edna's sprawling ranch style home.

After their meal, Edna turned on the TV so they could watch Lawrence Welk. It was a habit she'd slipped into during the judge's most recent dinner visits. Edna loved Welk's champagne music and she was wild about Dick Dale, who sang and played the saxophone. It was her favorite program on her favorite station – her station, now that Coleman Wright was gone. She watched after it like she'd been entrusted with the complete Cartier line.

Over the past four months, Winston Garland, recently retired from the superior court bench, had become a regular Saturday night dinner guest. He too was widowed — there were suspicious circumstances to his wife's drowning in her bathtub, but the judge was cleared in the investigation — and enjoyed the company of someone like Edna who shared his sense of loss. The relationship had been confined to friendly conversation, which suited Edna just fine. Lately, however, she'd picked up signs that Judge Garland might be tiring of just talk. He'd become touchy-feely upon greeting her of late. Edna was after all, an attractive, well-kept woman; a real catch, all things considered. Edna was proud of the fact that, even at sixty-eight, she still had the legs of a Vegas showgirl. She credited extensive hiking of the trails along the Mesa for maintaining the definition in her legs. It had been more than two years since her husband's massive heart attack (at age seventy) but as Edna was quick to inform inquiring minds — mostly her two daughters — "I'm not ready to jump in the sack with just anyone."

"...The lovely Lennon Sisters join us with their rendition of 'Getting to Know You' from Rodgers and Hammerstein's 'The King and I'...Girls..."

Without warning, the black and white picture on Edna's ancient Philco TV turned to snow. The delightful harmony of the Lennon Sisters was replaced by a hissing sound that reminded her of rushing water. "Oh, heavens!" Edna said. "The TV has finally gone on the blink. I just knew it was going to happen any day. You know Philco has stopped making them."

"It's not the TV," the judge said, first clearing his throat and then draining his glass and holding it up for another.

"There's no signal coming from your station, Edna. Haven't you ever experienced this before?"

"Unfortunately, too often. I don't pay my engineers very much. They don't have personalities. They're not good representatives of the station. You can bet my chief engineer is going to hear about this. This is deplorable."

The interruption lasted more than a minute before Edna, her eyes darting between the TV and her station hot phone. Finally, she picked up the phone and frantically awaited an answer. It never came. "Something's happened. Orrin Burdette is embarrassing me, Winston."

It was the first time Edna had called her guest by his first name. He made a mental note to file it under the heading of progress. "I wouldn't panic just yet," he told her.

As suddenly as it had disappeared, the picture on Edna's screen returned. "Oh, thank goodness," she sighed and slumped onto her couch. But in the next instant she felt her breath leave her. "My God, this isn't ..."

On the screen, a naked black man with tattoos masquerading as arms was cavorting on a bed with two naked women; one of them white, the other, black.

"It appears the Lennon Sisters have changed costumes," the judge said, his eyes fixed on the screen.

Edna's face turned pale and her eyes widened the size of sand dollars. "What in heaven's...?" She sat up straight and grabbed at her heart with both hands. "They...they're... having sex on my station."

For a minute Edna joined the judge in silence. All that could be heard were the sounds of raucous sex coming from her Philco.

It wasn't until the naked trio switched positions on the bed that the judge turned to Edna.

"I'll be damned," he said. "It's a skin flick. Somebody flipped the wrong switch or something."

Edna's face suddenly turned scarlet. "Could it be somebody's idea of a joke? It is, don't you think?"

"Afraid so."

Edna's body stiffened. "Whoever is responsible must pay, Winston. You'll see to that, won't you?"

"You have my word," he said placing his arm around her shoulders and pulling her close.

CHAPTER 3

Sylvia Miranda — Cha Cha to her friends because of the salsa moves she'd introduced to her touchdown celebrations as a Santa Barbara High School football cheerleader — was at home watching *The Dodge Dance Party* with her parents only because she'd recently broken up with her boyfriend, Zeke Clayton. Zeke, who was the Don's star quarterback, had been cheating on Cha Cha with a cheerleading rival from Ventura High, a safe thirty miles south of Santa Barbara. She'd caught them making out in the balcony of the Granada theatre during a sneak preview of *Lawrence of Arabia*. Cha Cha snuck up on the lovebirds in the dark and blasted them with a fire extinguisher. She never once regretted getting caught by the manager and having to pay for the damage with money she earned serving ice cream at Fosters' Freeze.

"Holy moly!" Cha Cha said under her breath as the picture on her TV switched to a close up of a black guy's extremely large piece. She sat straight up from her reclined position on the family room couch.

Cha Cha's mother, Maria Consuela, sprung from her mahogany recliner, where she'd been knitting peacefully awaiting the appearance of Larry Hooper, the piano player with the big baritone voice. She was advancing on the TV controls when Cha Cha's father, Ignacio shouted. *"Esperate!* "

"Mary mother of God, we can't watch this," Maria Consuela said, her eyes riveted on the screen. "It's sinful."

Ignacio had just knocked off a six-pack of Tecate in despair over a particularly bad week, in which he'd failed to convince a long list of prospective customers that he was a landscaper, not a dime-a-dozen, blow-and-go Mexican gardener. Fueled by the cervesas, Ignacio leaped from his position at the other end of the couch and grabbed his wife by her arm. *"Esperate!* Wait!"

"My God!" Cha Cha's mother shouted as she turned toward her husband, her deep-set brown eyes shooting daggers at him. "How could you allow our daughter to watch this? *Esta muy malo.* Turn it off! *Pronto!*"

"Esperate!" Ignacio barked again.

"Sylvia," Maria Consuela, said. *"Vete tu cuarto.* You will not watch this."

"But Mama, I'm eighteen now."

"Caramba!" Maria Consuela snatched up the sweater she'd been working on and stormed out of the room, leaving behind a tangled trail of yarn and a tidal wave of obscenities.

"Don't wake up my brothers with all that noise," Ignacio hollered.

Cha Cha didn't acknowledge her mother's departure. She remained glued to the TV, which is why she suddenly gasped. She turned to her father. "Do you see what I see, Papa?"

"Que? What?"

"The writing on the screen."

"My English no so good after too many cervezas," Ignacio said, his bloodshot eyes never leaving the screen.

"It says, 'Courtesy of the Class of '62, SMHS'."

"So what?" Ignacio said, popping open another Tecate.

"What a giant R.F.!" Cha Cha said.

"What?" Ignacio said.

Cha Cha and her father watched the remainder of the twelve-minute skin flick in silence. The only sound permeating the family room was that of three people speaking the language of sex. It reminded Cha Cha of a lesson on vowels. When the film finally ended she got up from the couch and announced she was changing the channel.

"Esperate!" Ignacio said. He wanted to watch the credits.

Cha Cha had no choice but to wait her father out. She jabbed her finger at a half-empty bowl of popcorn, only to have one of the credits capture her attention: Produced and distributed by Virgin Valley Pictures, Reseda, California. Her mind raced. She'd come across that name before. Try as she might she couldn't recall the first time.

CHAPTER 4

Police Chief Franklin McWorter was happy to have his dinner interrupted by word he was wanted on the telephone. It was 9:30PM and he'd just finished a flavorless chicken cordon bleu at La Cumbre Country Club's annual "New Members Night", a gentlemanly social designed for new members to bond with old. The phone call allowed him a respite from the nauseating chatter of new member Jeffery Baldwin, the do-nothing son of a successful commercial developer and an insufferable wine aficionado.

It had been all Chief McWorter could do to keep his attention from wandering while Baldwin rambled on about the "exquisite Cabs produced by the Napa Valley winery, the Brentwood Cellars."

"For fullness, harmony, balance and richness of taste," Baldwin preached, "you can't touch Brentwood's 1960 Cab. If you'll recall, we had a warm spring that year which allowed the grapes to stay on the vines longer. That translates to a more complete flavor. It was an extraordinary vintage that produced fruit of incredible color, depth and concentration, with intense tannin structure."

The chief responded with a wry smile. "Just goes to show you how people's tastes differ. If I want tannin' I head for Palm Springs." Baldwin excused himself immediately after the remark.

The call was from an overexcited Sergeant Caldwell, who was filling in as the night watch commander.

"You'll never believe this, Chief."

"Try me."

"Are you ready for a skin flick airing on Channel Three?"

"What?"

"One minute I'm watching champagne bubbles blowin', the next, some black dude with enough gold in his teeth to support the currency in some third world countries is getting a blow job to die for."

"Explain yourself, dammit, Sergeant."

"I'm talking about a guy with a dick the size of one of those ICBMs they launch at Vandenburg. And, he's sticking it in not one, but two women – a black and a white.

When the white gal's in the middle it reminds me of those cookies my kids are always screaming for. It's on my TV right this minute and judging from the volume of calls coming into dispatch, it's on everyone's TV in the whole damn town. And how tough do you think it's going to be to find the perpetrator when a message at the bottom of the screen says it's courtesy of this year's seniors at San Marcos High?"

Chief McWorter cleared his throat. "Damn punk high school kids. Fuckin' up another of my weekends."

"You gotta admit it's creative, Chief," Sergeant Caldwell laughed. "Jesus, you should see the booty on this black chick! Looks like someone blew those cheeks up with a fuckin' bicycle pump."

"I'll show you creative, Sergeant. You want a lead; I'll give you one. The San Marcos High class of '62 is having its senior party at this very moment."

"They are?"

"At the Coral Casino, across from the Biltmore."

"How do you know this, sir?"

"I'm paid to know these things. That's why I'm the chief and you're not. Besides, my daughter was invited. Some jerk off who came to the door with his fly open. I hope the bastard is in on this."

"If he is, we'll nail him, boss."

"Turn off your damned TV, Sergeant and call the Coral Casino. Tell the manager I'll be there in fifteen minutes. Have Brenda dispatch two units to the TV station. Get a forensics guy on it too. Have him dust the place floor to ceiling. And have four units meet me in front of the Coral Casino. Make Harmon the back up. We're going to catch us a prankster or two. Is that understood, Sergeant?"

"Affirmative, Chief."

"Smart ass pimply faced delinquents. They have no idea who they're fucking with."

Shortly after 9:45PM Wayne Preston told his prom date he had to go to the bathroom. A wild-haired charter member of San Marcos High's surfing clique, Preston had spent the last two days of high school reveling in the distinction of being named "least likely to succeed" in a school yearbook stunt that got past the faculty advisor.

Instead of going to the bathroom, Preston slipped unnoticed into a pool maintenance closet that had a small porthole-like window. It was the only safe harbor he could find.

Wayne's date was Hillary Fredrickson, the foxiest girl in the junior class. She had an ass so fine Wayne thought it should be in some museum someplace. And for the senior party she wore a powder blue strapless dress that showed more cleavage than Wayne figured was legal in California. The minute he laid eyes on her Wayne started boning up. He was certain Hillary's father was hip to his condition by the way he kept staring at his crotch as he presented his daughter a pink corsage when he picked her up. It wasn't the first time something like that had happened to Wayne. During the Valentine's dance his junior year Janet Nyborg playfully accused him of packing a firearm after she'd sat on his lap during a break in the music.

From the moment of his arrival at the senior party Wayne sported a hard on that could have doubled as a hat rack. He was reluctant to get close to Hillary for fear he'd embarrass himself. He decided to combat his problem head on, electing to do some weed in the hopes it would relax his monkey.

He'd just taken his first drag when the cops arrived. He could see everything through a peephole in the closet door. Chief McWorter, decked out in his full dress blues and flashing what resembled Elvis sideburns, stood on the top step that lead down to the pool and portable dance floor. Two officers on either side flanked him. Wayne recognized the chief from a school assembly on the evils of drugs. He'd been the main speaker. Wayne remembered taking pride in the fact he and a handful of buddies were stoned on grass during the presentation.

Chief McWorter held his service revolver high as he and his posse descended on the class of '62. "Everybody freeze!" he shouted. "Don't any of you disrespectful punks move. I have questions and I want lots of answers."

The command set off a stampede right out of a *Wagon Train* episode – students and chaperones alike. They bolted for exits in every direction. Two guys in white tuxedos with pint

bottles of Jim Beam sticking out of the pockets climbed a twenty-foot fountain that resembled Neptune, and jumped onto the balcony above the pool. Wayne assumed they made their escape from there by jumping down onto the tennis courts. Several girls dove into the indoor section of the pool and vanished out the open-air wing, which served as a gateway to the ocean. Pink corsages bobbing on the water's surface were the only traces they left behind.

Everybody vanished so quickly that Chief McWorter and his men could do nothing. Wayne Preston would later tell his buddies, "The cops froze like they were ice sculptures."

Hoping the smell of dope wouldn't attract McWorter and company Wayne took another hit. He suddenly felt he needed a bigger high. Less than a minute after the cops' arrival the place was near empty, except for one. Wayne could see Penny Sexton crumpled on the floor next to the water cooler. Penny was holding her shoes in one hand and a drink of some kind in the other. Her head was in her lap and she was crying.

Wayne felt his pulse quicken as he watched the chief approach her.

"Get up!" he said. "We want to talk to you, young lady. I want to know where you got that booze."

Penny didn't respond right away. She just kept crying. Then, as the chief leaned down to take her by the arm, she began to wail. "I hate him! Do you hear me? I hate him. If it weren't for him I'd have been homecoming queen. Do you hear that? Queen. The bastard. Can you believe Linda Dalby got it? The skag. It should have been me. Ladies and gentlemen...please greet Queen Penny and her court."

Penny wasn't done. She began singing. "... I hate Paris in the spring time, I hate Paris in the fall, I hate the bastard any old time..." Suddenly, she stopped and began laughing hysterically.

Wayne heard the chief order one of his men to drive her home. "Imagine having a daughter like that," he said as the officer scooped Penny from the floor.

In the same instant Wayne witnessed Whitney Crawford, the class "whipping boy," rush through the Coral Casino's main entrance. He was dressed in wrinkled khakis, a flowered Hawaiian shirt, and had on his standard Jerry Lewis-like horn-rimmed glasses. He was out of breath.

"Hold it right there," Chief McWorter shouted, pointing his revolver at Whitney. "What's your name, son?"

"Whitney."

"Got a last name, son?"

"Crawford, sir."

Wayne couldn't believe how meek Whitney was acting. "Show some balls," he whispered.

"Why aren't you dressed in a penguin outfit like the rest?" the chief said. "You been hanging out at the TV station?"

"TV station? No, sir."

"What's your reason for being here, then?"

Whitney appeared to Wayne to be shaking as he spoke. "I don't have a date, sir. I was sitting at home listening to my police scanner and I heard the call go out for units to the Coral Casino. I just came to see what was happening. Honest, I don't date, sir."

Chief McWorter ordered another of his officers to take Whitney to a squad car for further questioning.

"I don't even like girls," Whitney said as he was being dragged away.

What happened next made Wayne Preston think the marijuana was suddenly getting to him like never before. A partially clad young couple appeared arm-in-arm at the opposite end of the dance floor from where the chief had confronted Whitney. It was obvious from the sand residue on what little they were wearing that they'd come from he beach. The boy was shoeless and his ribbed shirt was open to his navel. He was holding his cummerbund in his right hand. The girl's flowing blonde hair was wet and matted with sand. She was wearing only her bra and a slip that was badly torn at the hemline. She carried her heels in her hand.

"Daddy," the girl said as she approached the chief on unsteady legs. "Wha…are you doing here?" she said, giggling as she spoke.

"Arrest this boy!" the chief shouted, placing the barrel of his revolver under the boy's chin. "And you," he said to the girl. "You're grounded for life, young lady."

The girl tried to reach out and grab the chief's uniform jacket but instead pitched forward, almost losing her balance. "But …Daddy," she said. "It was my first…very first time. I swear. Now, you don't want me to have bad… memories of my first time, do you?"

Wayne's chin dropped as he watched Chief McWorter direct another of his posse to take his daughter home.

"And get a robe on her for God sakes," he yelled. "There must be one in this den of sin somewhere."

CHAPTER 5

Janet Nyborg was relieved her grandparents were going out to Smorgy King, as was their Saturday evening ritual. They also planned on taking in Jimmy Stewart's latest, *Mr. Hobbs Takes a Vacation*, which Janet regarded as a bonus. She was expecting an important phone call and was pleased she'd be able to take it in private – privacy being a precious commodity when four people are sharing a three room mobile home. She also liked the idea of having one-on-one time with her infant son, Lance.

"I'll do ironing for you Grams, if you leave stuff out for me," Janet said, as Ruth and Joe Nyborg were about to exit the front door.

"It's not necessary, darlin'," Ruth said. "Just take good care of the little mister and give him a good night kiss for me."

If little Lance hadn't come along Janet would be enjoying her San Marcos High senior class party this very evening instead of waiting by the phone for a call from a friend who was graduating. When Janet's parents learned she was pregnant in August of 1961 they notified school administrators. A day later the school principal told Janet she couldn't attend school during the calendar year of her pregnancy. Private schools were not an option on her parents' salaries; they were both supermarket clerks. Without even consulting Janet, her parents chose to ship her off to family hundreds of miles away in Weed, California: population three thousand. Weed is a lumber town located on the western slopes of Mt. Shasta in Northern California. Joe and Ruth live in a trailer park just outside the city limits. Ruth was happy to have Janet come stay with her; Joe wasn't.

As he followed Ruth out the door Joe said, "Make it a night of firsts, Janet. Try cleaning up your room and giving the telephone a rest while we're gone."

"I'm planning on using the time to practice concealing my boobs from your lecherous stares," Janet wanted to say, but held her tongue.

Janet was a long-legged, blonde who'd kept her hair in a ponytail since the first grade. She'd grown into a moderately attractive teen with bright green eyes. Long before she experienced zits, she developed movie star-like breasts, "Mount Janet's," boys called them. As she got older her two biggest assets became her single biggest problem. Every teenage boy with a pulse and a pecker wanted to get into her drawers. Compounding Janet's problem was her inexplicable inability to say no to sex. She once did the co-captains of the football team on the same night rather than say no to one. She viewed saying "no" as a punishable offense.

It didn't come as a great surprise to Janet or any of her girlfriends that she couldn't determine who'd gotten her pregnant. She'd been having regular sex with half a dozen guys; Wayne Preston, Reno Parris and Edgar Peoples among them. None of the boys volunteered to come forward for testing and, after numerous heated discussions, Janet convinced her parents not to pursue legal options.

Shortly after 11:00PM, as Janet was biting a last defenseless fingernail, the phone rang. She leaped from the couch and took it after the first ring.

"Tell me all about it," she said without a hello. "Tell me. Tell me." Her energetic greeting was followed by a brief silence. "Wait. Who is this?" she finally said. Another pause. "You fucking pervert. Go stick your limp dick in a blender and do every girl within a hundred square miles a giant favor." She slammed the receiver against the wall, taking a chip out of the plaster that she knew she'd pay hell for with Grandpa Joe.

Janet was still angry when she went to bed – mad at who hadn't called. She lay awake, holding out hope, until she heard her grandparents return. At the sound of the front door closing she slammed her fist into her pillow, then cried herself to sleep.

CHAPTER 6

A weathered portable storage shed out back of his badly rusted 19-foot silver Gulfstream trailer was the last place Reno Parris planned to look for his suitcase. If it wasn't there he'd do without it – just stuff his clothes in a pillowcase. Reno couldn't remember the last time he'd used the damn thing. It was probably when he moved to Quincy two years ago to take the 4-to-7PM sports talk slot on KPSC radio, the only AM station in Plumas County, an hour and a half from Lake Tahoe.

Even though it's the county seat, Quincy doesn't have enough people to require a stoplight. Little wonder Reno had so much trouble getting callers for his radio show. Not that he cared. He'd much rather rant for three hours about how professional athletes are grossly overpaid than listen to some liquored-up caller concoct a fantasy trade where the Giants would send Barry Bonds and a player to be named later to the Yankees for George Kostanza.

From day one Reno, already eccentric with his thick, gray goatee and shoulder length salt-and-pepper hair was encouraged by station management to be opinionated. "Over the top," his boss labeled it. They promoted his show, as "Parris is Burning." It was KPSC's ratings leader since Reno's first broadcast when he claimed he could name at least one queer on every major league roster. Reno made it clear he was speaking from experience, having played twelve years professionally as a shortstop-turned-catcher. He didn't volunteer that he'd never made it past Double A ball.

A half a century and close to fifty pounds ago Reno was labeled, by those who should know, the best baseball prospect to come out of Santa Barbara – better than Eddie Mathews. His greatest claim to fame, however, was beating out Bull Durham director Ron Shelton for all Channel League honors as a senior. Shelton played for rival Santa Barbara High. Reno spent his whole career in the minors chasing the outside curve and anything in a skirt.

Clearly he had some reservations about attending the class of '62's first reunion. How many names, not to mention faces, could he remember from those days – maybe a half dozen? And how many times would he be made to feel worse than vomit catching up with classmates who'd served in Vietnam while he was seeing action as the Ventura Angels' lead off man? But, if the reunion really could help chase the demons that had cursed the class of '62 like the organizer promised, he'd be there with bells on.

Reno had more reason than most to believe in the curse. How else could he rationalize such a disappointing life? Reno often joked he could measure his life by the numbers: (12) years in the minors, (6) failed marriages to (4) women, two dozen (24) jobs – after baseball, a Chapter 7, and a quadruple bypass? "Add up the numbers," he would say, "divide by your age, and you have your 'fuck up' factor. I'm sitting on 1.2 per year."

Technically, Reno never officially graduated from San Marcos if a diploma is required as proof. After the Lawrence Welk *skin flick* caper, the Santa Barbara Unified School District board of trustees ordered all diplomas invalid and didn't issue new ones until two months later when Chief McWorter finally backed off on his investigation. Reno never applied for the valid certificate.

There was another reason for Reno to point his beat up Chevy Tacoma in the direction of Santa Barbara – Holly Murchison. He'd discovered from organizer Dee Dee Wellborn's Evite that Holly's name was on the small list of possible attendees. One of the great mysteries in Reno's life was why, a week after he'd signed with the L.A. Angels and was on top of the world she broke up with him by way of a postcard. To this day Reno remembers every written word:

Dear Reno,

It's sad our lives have taken different turns, plus me being Catholic and all. I wish you well in baseball. Watch out for those groupies. I loved our time togehter as steadies. As for me, I'm looking forward to pledging shortly after I enroll at Berkeley.

Holly

Reno hoped the reunion would finally bring closure to his first great romance. For that reason he'd decided not to invite Pearl along, even if his absence meant she'd likely get hit-on by every horny redneck from Reno to Kings Beach. Pearl tended bar at Plumas Pines tavern, located just east of the Quincy city limits. It was strictly a local's place. Had been ever since four Hells Angels out of Fresno required hospitalization a few years back after sexually assaulting the manager's girlfriend while she was sitting at the bar having a drink. About a dozen locals swarmed the bikers and beat them practically to death.

Pearl, who'd only recently turned fifty, was what Reno referred to as a pistol. She had flaming red hair and a temper to match. She claimed the dubious distinction of having two ex-husbands who'd been granted restraining orders against her. She'd learned to kick-box in her early twenties — competed professionally until she fractured a foot — and that's how she defended herself when she got in a mess. Fortunately for Reno, he'd never experienced Pearl's wrath. All he knew about her was she had tits big enough to land commercial jets and every time she fucked it seemed like it was for the national championship. She also spoke his language, "politically incorrect."

Pearl wasn't happy about Reno's leaving town to party without her. "Don't let that pecker of yours get nostalgic," she'd warned. The only reason she didn't put up a stronger protest was that she hoped he'd better be able to focus on ending his run of bad luck. She didn't know about Holly Murchison.

CHAPTER 7

Deep down, Dee Dee Wellborn knew the manager of the Sea Breeze motel would panic. But once the day of the reunion finally arrived she'd figured she was home free.

The Sea Breeze was a sixty-year-old, two-story structure that was badly in need of a facelift. With its orange stucco exterior and blue tile roof, it looked like a monument to a can of Orange Crush. In the interest of low maintenance, the owner had black topped the property as if living plants were a threat to the safety of his guests. The twenty-four-unit motel, which could only have received its three star rating by the owner greasing somebody's palm, couldn't have caught a sea breeze with an industrial vacuum given that it was located in a valley bordered by giant oak trees, some three miles east of the ocean on upper State Street. It was, however, one of only a handful of motels in town with an adjoining activity center.

Anthony Castello, the Sea Breeze's manager called Dee Dee shortly before noon with word that the reunion party was in jeopardy. She was getting her nails done at the time and split three when she slammed the phone down. Dee Dee desperately wanted the night to be a success. She considered it her "coming-out-of-shit" party. She'd gone to great lengths to look her best for the occasion. Only recently she'd traded her Connie Francis hairstyle of five decades for something semi-spiked out of *Vogue*. She'd also shed twenty pounds to a size twelve on a diet of soymilk and rice cakes. She was quick to boast that she now weighed exactly the same as she did when she finished second in the shot put at the State CIF finals.

Dee Dee arrived at Anthony Castello's tiny Sea Breeze office less than a half hour after she'd received his call. She found him sitting at his desk staring at a blank computer screen. He had a big circle of sweat under each arm. He had B.O. that smelled like eucalyptus. Anthony was a slight Italian man with big bushy white eyebrows. He had more hair sticking out of his crooked nose than he had on his head. His back was slightly hunched from what appeared to be an arthritic condition. Dee Dee figured him to be in his mid-seventies. He'd managed small, single-owner motels from Santa Monica north since coming to the U.S. from Northern Sicily twenty-five years ago.

Dee Dee practically had to beg Anthony to explain his phone call.

His voice quivered when he spoke. "The owner feeling very much pressure from…how you say…pressure groups? He say they tell him if he permits the party everybody boy-got him – "

"Boycott," Dee Dee said.

Anthony's eyelids twitched as he spoke. "They say all vendors drop him like drug habit."

"Like a bad habit," Dee Dee said.

"Something like that. Whatever…it no good."

After considerable arm-twisting, Dee Dee convinced Anthony that another thousand dollars toward the activity center rental would ease his boss' fear of reprisal.

"It's big gamble, but you make it okay," Anthony said, smiling for the first time since Dee Dee arrived.

No sooner had Dee Dee finished administering CPR to the reunion party than Anthony's boss called him again, saying he'd been warned by Police Chief Franklin McWorter, Jr. – the son of – that his men might raid the party for no good reason other than it was the class of '62. Dee Dee countered the news by offering Anthony another thousand dollars. She quickly calculated she'd have to charge her classmates and additional sixty-five bucks to cover her unforeseen outlay. It might not fly with everybody, Dee Dee reasoned, but she was confident she could make it so Anthony wouldn't know if he got short changed. After all, Dee Dee had come very close to beating an embezzlement charge for something far bigger than this.

She'd spent ten years in prison for applying her creative accounting skills to her job as bookkeeper for a local construction company. The four million dollars she'd re-directed from Ellsworth Construction over a five-year period in the early eighties went to finance her third husband's Gold Cup hydroplane racing team. It turned out to be a wasted effort. Her husband was slapped with a lifetime suspension by the American Power Boat Association. The charge; secretly trying to run a rocket engine in his number one boat, *Miss Double D*.

No fewer than three shrinks – spanning three decades– had independently concluded that any and all of Dee Dee's problems – legal and personal – were the direct result of her obsession with pleasing men. It started with her need to present straight As to her father as early as the second grade. That was followed in high school by her need to give blowjobs like they were on seasonal close out.

Her current shrink believes the fallout from the Lawrence Welk *skin flick* caper accelerated that obsession as an adult. The shrink's theory is that Dee Dee believed she'd failed her principal, John Nesbitt. Because she was the senior class president she held herself personally responsible for his being exiled by the superintendent over the *skin flick* caper. Dee Dee, however, still holds firm to the belief that her problems are solely the result of the *skin flick curse*.

Just a year after high school she found a husband. She chose to make him money rather than babies, by becoming a gambler. She had some early success at the casinos in Las Vegas and Reno – mostly at poker. Then she switched to betting the ponies at Santa Anita and Hollywood Park and in a matter of months went through all their cash. For husband number two she raised funds for a bogus charity by holding bake sales and pocketing one hundred percent of the profits. She quit as soon as the law began sniffing around. By her third wedding, Dee Dee was desperate to succeed at marriage.

Dee Dee had always been good with numbers, going back as far as high school. Few of her peers have likely forgotten how she won the race for senior class president in a monumental upset. A number of ballots cast by students in her opponent's homeroom had mysteriously disappeared. The ballots weren't discovered for over a year, after Dee Dee had left school. Not surprisingly, narcotics sniffing dogs belonging to the county sheriff found them when they'd run afoul of a marijuana scent in a trench located a stone's throw from the UCSB economics building. Dee Dee's dad was a professor there.

Before leaving the Sea Breeze to run last-minute errands, Dee Dee, accompanied by Anthony, made a final check of the activity center, which was really nothing more than a fifteen-hundred square-foot room that featured floor-to-ceiling fake wood paneling, a single mounted deer's head, a faded twenty-by-thirty poster of President Bush and a Coke machine that Anthony said hadn't worked since Bush 41.

She wanted to make sure the tables were set up correctly and that there was enough room for the four-person band she'd hired.

"The caterer will be here at six o'clock," she said to Anthony.

"If they show."

"Oh, please don't say that, Anthony." Dee Dee crossed herself.

At first Anthony looked away. After a time he turned back. "It be okay," he said, softly. "I know this reunion important to you. We make happen, okay?"

Dee Dee took Anthony's small, sweaty hands in hers. "You don't know, Anthony. Everyone in this class has paid an unbelievable price for someone's stupid prank. Lives have been changed and careers altered by that single mindless incident. Just look at me." She pointed a finger at her chest. "Would I have gone to prison and gotten all these God awful coiled Cobra tattoos on my arms if I hadn't been made by some mysterious force to feel I'd failed a whole community? And still, nobody knows who did it. It's so crazy. All I know is the class of '62 – all 440 of us – has been this town's black sheep for decades." Dee Dee wiped at her tears. "Tonight, even though there aren't many of us, we're going to gather in brother-and sisterhood and say to one another, 'it wasn't our fault'. It's going to be an evening of cleansing, Anthony."

Anthony asked Dee Dee if she'd like some water. She waved her hand, no. "When I was in prison, Anthony, I did a lot of reading. Have you ever heard of Sun Tzu?"

Anthony scratched his forehead. "The car?"

"No, no." Dee Dee smiled for the first time. "He was a great Chinese military strategist twenty-five hundred years ago. His concepts have been passed along and recently applied to business and self-improvement. Count the enemy's weaknesses and then exploit them; it's that simple. It's what I trying to do with this reunion party. I want to confront our demons when they're least expecting it."

Anthony listened intently.

"You can learn all about Sun Tzu online at *Sonshi.com*. That's the Japanese translation for Sun Tzu."

Anthony waved his arms like he was asking for a time out. "I no follow," he said.

"The only thing you need to know, Anthony is that we have you to thank for making it happen. No one else had the guts to book us. You should be proud."

Anthony stepped away and exited the activity center without explanation. Dee Dee battled more tears. Several minutes passed before Anthony returned. He was holding in his hand the two thousand dollars in cash Dee Dee had given him.

"It's by me," he said, handing her the cash.

"On me, you mean, Anthony?"

"Something like that."

More tears. "Oh, what can I ever do to please…ah, thank you, Anthony?" Dee Dee left before Anthony could answer.

CHAPTER 8

Zeke Clayton studied his image in the rearview mirror as he worked through Malibu traffic in his burgundy Mercedes coup. He liked what he saw: a chin cut from granite, penetrating steel gray eyes, distinguished silver hair, rich bronze tan, a ten thousand dollar gold chain showing off a neck that was remarkably free of wrinkles, and– he reached up and twisted the mirror to reflect his passenger – a lights out gorgeous blonde, half his age, with tits as firm as cantaloupes. Life was good for the head of Clayton Pictures, as long as he didn't think about turning sixty-seven next month. When such thoughts did occur he'd combat them by rushing to the studio's gym and hopping on a treadmill for six miles or sixty minutes, whichever came first. "That will hold that *Father Time* bastard," he was fond of saying. Privately Zeek thought of himself as the poster boy for Hollywood success.

One hand on the wheel, Zeke dialed a number on his cell. "Enrique!" he barked, hoping to compensate for the wind noise. It was the only thing he had against convertibles.

"You got that lame dick film commission guy softened up for me? If not I'm going to check your expense report with a fucking telescope, the kind that lets you see naked women on Mars." In an effort to retain some of Zeke's attention, Lonnie the blonde, playfully dragged her hand across his crotch. Zeke winced. "Stop it some more," his lips read.

"Could be a problem, boss," Enrique Zendejas said. "He's getting pressure from that fuck ball police chief who says crowd control issues at our locations would raise havoc with his budget. Translated, it means too many cops on overtime."

"Chrissakes, Enrique, we're not filming a world war. Just a medium budget movie about a skin flick that made it onto the public airwaves."

"The chief figures there would be a ton of protestors. I'm telling you, boss, the people in this town still have a major fuckin' hard on for the class of '62. Even after all these years."

"Maybe I should book some face time with the chief?"

"Not a bad idea. Go right to the source."

"See if he's available for dinner tonight. Book the El Encanto on the Riviera. Tell him I have a fond recollection of his father, the fuck."

With a smile in his voice Enrique said, "I'll work on him."

"Did you tell the film commission fuck how much was in it for him?"

"He said he wasn't in the habit of taking bribes. Arrogant S.O.B."

"Sounds like I'll have to let him beat me today. Maybe give him a stroke a hole. We're set for Sandpiper at 2:40PM, aren't we?"

"That's affirmative, boss. I invited the mayor like you asked but she doesn't do golf. So I invited a fellow named Don Iverson: biggest residential developer in the county. Thought you could use another smart business man in your corner."

"Nice work, Enrique. You're still the best location director in the business."

"And, the lowest paid." Enrique laughed.

"One more thing, *amigo*," Zeke said. "See if you can drop by that reunion party tonight and line me up some class member contacts. I might need their lobby as well."

"Will do," Enrique said.

"You know how bad I want to make this picture in Santa Barbara. No other location will do. Make it happen, baby!"

Lonnie, apparently thinking Zeke was talking to her, reached over and delicately unzipped his fly. For the next ninety seconds Zeke's Mercedes weaved north along the Pacific Coast Highway like it was negotiating an oil slick.

People in the film industry have long maintained that Zeke Clayton is both a creative genius and a great deal maker. He's won three Oscars for Best Picture and two more for Best Director. In thirty years he'd built Clayton Pictures into a mega-million dollar company – privately held. Many of the same industry people will tell you he's a flaming asshole, as well. He's known as "The Burbank Bully" among many who've worked for him.

"His only loyalty is to his penis," one of his leading ladies said of him in a recent *Vanity Fair*.

Zeke Clayton had a history of signing stars whose careers were in free-fall to bargain basement contracts, then trashing them after they'd contributed to another of his successes. His properties are so consistently good that they become hits no matter what actor or actress had the lead. Lana Turkel, won best actress for *Death After Dark*, and she'd been out of work five years. Her asking price spiked with the Oscar, so Zeke let her go.

He built his empire by structuring percentage deals with those who helped back his early projects. He took practically nothing for writing and directing *Glory Daze* about a pot-smoking platoon of U.S. infantrymen who became Vietnam War legends for their kill ratio, but who, to a man, battled post war drug addiction that ruined each of their lives. Zeke got thirty percent of the film's gross against expenses. The picture made a hundred million.

Zeke Clayton knew he wanted to be a big time Hollywood player as far back as high school. His father, Andrew Clayton, ran a Montecito-based law firm that represented mostly showbiz clients, so Zeke got the taste of celebrity early. At sixteen, he got a push in that direction from his dad. Andrew enrolled him in summer classes at Brooks Film Institute – the top film school in the country. He learned the basics of both still photography and film.

A pro-football career was supposed to have preceded entry into the movie business. Zeke had earned a full ride to USC as a strong-armed quarterback who'd guided Santa Barbara High School to the CIF Southern Section Championship game against Centennial High of L.A. Santa Barbara lost 21-7, never scoring after Zeke went down with a hyper-extended knee in the second quarter.

"Super Zeke," as a local sports columnist labeled him, had been on track to have starred for San Marcos High, but got the boot from the school's principal halfway through his sophomore year. He was caught hiding a remote controlled film camera – first of its kind – in the shower room of the girl's gym. The student who made the discovery and linked it to Zeke was afraid she'd be harmed if she ratted on him, so it was somehow left to Linda Dalby, the class vice-president to go to the principal. It was ironic that Linda took the lead, considering the school's internal investigation of the matter turned up a film in which she and two cheerleaders appeared singing, *Big Girl's Don't Cry* while soaping each other. Linda's parents filed a sexual harassment suit against Zeke, which his dad managed to get thrown out court.

Zeke spent his remaining high school years bashing his old school at every opportunity. In a Santa Barbara News Press article that was published prior to the CIF championship game, Zeke called San Marcos a training center for incompetent teachers and coaches. "They're head coach is a math teacher. That says it all," he was quoted as saying. "They belong coaching flag football."

As a Trojan, Zeke failed to live up to his billing. A knee injury ended his career a week before his sophomore season. It wasn't a pre-season training injury that brought him down, but an enraged girlfriend who'd caught him screwing her roommate and chased him down the stairs of her apartment with a carving knife. Zeke caught an edge halfway down the stairs and tore his ACL in a fall that witnesses swear was the equal of a 3.4 earthquake.

CHAPTER 9

They'd circled the Sea Breeze motel a half-dozen times trying to make up their minds about taking a room. Cecil Shapiro and Vernon Goldstein, a pair of balding, bespectacled, philosophical bookends, were dead tired from an eight-hour drive from Las Vegas in their noisy Ford van. They both craved sleep. Being crooks at age seventy-eight and eighty-one respectively had its drawbacks.

"I'd give up sex for eight uninterrupted hours of sack time, Vernon."

Vernon laughed. "Like that would be a sacrifice. I've got sources who tell me you can't get it up with a forklift anymore."

Cecil shook his head. "You've been listening to Francis McCarthy, haven't you?"

Vernon smiled.

"She's loony. She makes that stuff up. You think I'm going to pull my instrument out for some crazy old bat. Besides, she's got such a cellulite problem caretakers are starting to find food crumbs in pockets on her thighs."

Vernon pulled the Ford Aerostar to a stop less than a hundred feet from the Sea Breeze's driveway. His eyes scanned the surrounding area. "Looks harmless to me," he said. "There's no coffee shop so there won't be any cops on break."

"You think of everything," Cecil said.

"I just think for the both of us, Cecil."

"What about freeway access, Vernon. We're a long way from anything resembling an on ramp."

"You watch too much TV, Cecil. That stuff's overrated. It's easier to get lost on surface streets. Ever see the cops in L.A. chasing somebody down a boulevard? It's why they're called freeway chases."

"If you say so, Vernon." Cecil tugged at the brim of his Nike golf cap and slumped in his seat like he was going to nap.

Vernon popped the driver door open and slowly, carefully got out. "Getting old is worse than not getting' any, Cecil."

"Tell me about it, Vernon."

Vernon took one last look in the direction of the motel office. "I'll check it out," he said. "While I'm gone you get on your cell and find us a storage unit where we can dump this stuff. Don't want to leave three hundred golf clubs sitting in this van over night."

Cecil pushed back his cap and sat up. "If you ask me we should store those *Power Stroke* drivers in the bleeping ocean. Just drive out to the wharf and start tossing them. Who's gonna buy a piece-of-shit club just because it's at a black market price? Vernon, the product isn't up to our standards. Think about it. Two hundred bucks for a driver with a club head that three out of ten times travels further than the ball."

"Jeez, already. That only happens if you over swing, Cecil. You know that."

"You know we should have lifted that shipment of *True Line* putters. Those things are red hot ever since Hampton Boyle went birdie, eagle, birdie to overtake Tiger at Augusta."

"You're the one with the bad back, Cecil. What was I supposed to do, carry those one hundred pound crates out of the shop myself? I'm not as athletic as I used to be."

"I hear you can't both shit and wipe yourself anymore, that it's down to one or the other."

"Well, you heard wrong, Cecil."

Cecil and Vernon had decided to become crooks almost five years ago to the day. Strangers, they were paired in the Saddleback Seniors Golf and Canasta Slam, which was played annually at the Papago Golf and Social Center in Scottsdale, Arizona. Vernon shot a 98 if you didn't count the penalty strokes and Mulligans, which Cecil did. Otherwise, Vernon would have posted low net and won a booklet of ten free meal coupons at the Sizzler of his choice.

Riding in the same cart, they got to talking and discovered they had lots in common: both were widowed, both were retired electricians, and both were barely making it on social security. Cecil worried his golf game was going to hell. He'd recently upgraded to one bedroom from a studio at the Willow Creek Jewish Senior Living Center and it had stressed his budget something awful. As a precaution, he'd cut back on his golf expenses, playing only five days a week.

As their friendship grew, their golfing buddies began calling them the "Punctuations." Slender with a long trunk and stubby legs, Vernon looked like an exclamation mark.

Cecil, on the other hand, was slight of build as well, but had a potbelly that made him look like a question mark.

In the five years the two of them had been burglarizing golf stores and pro shops throughout the western states, Vernon estimated they'd hauled in close to a million and a half dollars. Mostly they'd steal clubs, but lately they'd begun to branch out to include shoes and apparel. They had fences for the goods in eight states. Vernon credited the Internet for extending the reach of the business.

Cecil worried of late, however, that the law of averages was going to catch up to them. He threatened more than once to get out. Claimed that because of all the travel, he was missing the good things in life like Super Bingo Thursday at the Center.

While Vernon was taking care of registering, Cecil dutifully located a storage unit where they could drop off their Vegas haul.

"Room's are nice," Vernon said, getting behind the wheel of the Aerostar.

"Good," Cecil responded.

"Manager says he has no vacancy for the first time in years."

"That means we won't be nearly as conspicuous."

"But, what really pleased Vernon was that Cecil had apparently forgotten about the wharf dumping idea.

CHAPTER 10

Whitney Crawford sensed his eighty-eight year old mother was watching him from her living room rocker as he stood in front of the tall hallway mirror examining the gray Hickey Freeman suit he'd purchased for this very evening. She was pretending to watch Lawrence Welk re-runs on PBS – her Saturday night staple – but what she was really doing was inspecting him. It was difficult for Whitney to avoid his mother's prying eyes in a house that featured walls of glass. They lived in a gray Eichler home, one of a number of contemporary flat-roofed houses that first appeared in Santa Barbara subdivisions in the late fifties. Eichlers, as the homes quickly became known, were designed to promote an indoor-outdoor style of living. An atrium was at the center of every Eicheler design.

Any second, Whitney Crawford expected his mother's warning. He knew the routine all too well from so many years under the same roof with her.

"Be sure and take an overcoat, Whitney," Elizabeth Crawford said. "It can get so nippy at night, you know. Coastal fog always rolls in late this time of year."

For years it had angered Whitney that his mother refused to treat him as an adult. He'd constantly been reminded to: eat breakfast, brush his teeth, clean his room, make his bed, place his dirty clothes in the hamper, have something nice to say to everybody, and of course, the overcoat. Thanks to counseling he'd only recently learned to curb his anger. He'd come to accept that it was just his mother's method of self-validation. When Whitney's father died twenty years ago she lost her identity.

Whitney hadn't planned on living his whole life with his parents. He went to UCSB so he could stay at home, but he soon wished he'd gone away to school. Maybe if he'd found a girlfriend things would have been different. There was Emily Bentencourt in high school. They'd kissed once behind the cafeteria during the Harvest Moon dance, but Whitney got so worked up he jizzed all over himself. He had a wet spot in the crotch of his Levis the size of a soccer ball. Emily thought it was cute, but Whitney was so embarrassed he never asked her out again, or anyone for that matter.

Best he can remember Whitney had only three beds in his lifetime. His entire sophomore year of high school, he never got out of bed. He'd contacted mononucleosis so severe his doctor feared it might actually be malaria instead. Even when he was healthy, Whitney would never be confused with someone on a box of Wheaties. He stood no more than 5'8" and weighed maybe 150. His skin was always pasty white and he had no muscle tone – he'd made a career out of skipping gym class.

Whitney's only notable achievement in grades K thru 12 was making the debate team his last year at San Marcos. Actually, he was the first alternate. It was enough, however, to spawn a dream of becoming a lawyer like his Uncle Wendell. Then came the Lawrence Welk *skin flick* caper. Like everyone from the class of '62, Whitney was denied admission to all UC and state universities on the count of "extenuating circumstances" even though he carried a 3.8 GPA. That denial is what triggered Whitney's belief in a curse.

"How does this look, Mother?" Whitney said, modeling his suit. "It's my new power suit," he said, his lips turned up on one side like some TV bad guy.

"You look as if you're dressed for court, son. Isn't this supposed to be a party you're going to?"

"Oh, it's a party alright. But I've got some serious business to conduct as well."

"You're always so serious about everything. You haven't seen these people in so many years. Just go have fun, why don't you?"

"Any more parting advice?" Whitney said, giving his mother a kiss on the cheek.

Elizabeth took his arms in her outstretched hands. "Don't drink so much that people will notice you walk funny. They'll never stop asking you about your prosthesis."

"Christ! You had to remind me of that." Over time, walking with a "fake" leg, as he chose to call it, he'd gotten pretty good at concealing a limp. But his mother was right for once. As soon as he got some booze in him his navigation skills deteriorated.

Whitney acquired his limp in the Army. With California colleges removed from the mix –Whitney was certain it was Edna Pendleton Wright's strong lobby with the governor's office – and not able to afford out of state tuitions, he signed up for military duty in a strange protest, just before Vietnam got bad. During basic training at Fort Ord, he stepped in a foxhole during night maneuvers and broke his kneecap in a gazillion places. His leg had to be amputated.

For most of his adult life Whitney was quick to tell relatives and friends that his career was on target. Truth was, he worked for Target. In twenty-five years he'd gone from stock boy to assistant manager in the same store in Goleta, a small town just north of Santa Barbara.

"No one moves kitchen products like my store," he was proud of telling his mother.

While he was forced to put his dream of being a lawyer on hold for decades, Whitney persevered. He studied law online at *www.lawline.com*. It took him eight years of staying up into the early morning hours, but he finally graduated and passed his bar exam on the first try.

He was a bridesmaid too many times to count when it came to getting a job with an established Santa Barbara law firm. "Extenuating circumstances," he was told. So, five years ago, Whitney hung up a shingle of his own and started chasing ambulances. He marketed himself as the discount king of personal injury cases.

"Oops, forgot my ballots," Whitney said to his mother as he re-entered the house.

"Are you sure you're attending a reunion tonight, Whitney? You're not doing something kinky are you?" Elizabeth laughed, but not her son.

"The class of '62 has an important vote tonight, Mother. They just don't know it yet."

Whitney wished his mother good night a second time and closed the front door. He tilted his head back and rolled his eyes skyward and addressed the heavens. "I'm going to pry the fucking truth out of someone, so help me, God. Somebody is going to pay for the curse."

CHAPTER 11

The June 25th edition of KEYT's 6:15PM news had a different look: reporter Bill Hurley could be seen in living color by the few viewers who were fortunate to have colored sets. It was a significant technological advancement for a small market station like KEYT. A handful of network affiliates began broadcasting news and local events in the mid-fifties – among them WBAP in Fort Worth, WCCO in Minnesota and KRLA in Los Angeles – but they were slow to be joined by others.

What made KEYT's ascent into the ranks of color technology so unusual was that the station didn't own a color floor camera. It did possess a color slide chain, however, and a bright engineer in Orrin Burdette. Using a patchwork mirroring system, Orrin managed to rig the slide chain so that it performed like a color camera. It could only be operated from a fixed position, but it worked, as long as the person on camera didn't move around a lot. Orrin had completed a final trial of the system a week before he died.

While station personnel, from the general manager to the mail room superintendent expressed great pride in the fact KEYT was now among the color TV elite, many were privately embarrassed at the realization that what local viewers were discovering with their newfound color was the same old Bill Hurley.

Hurley managed to astonish even Edna Pendleton Wright on that historic first night, when he failed mention the colorcast or recognize his deceased co-worker. As always the news was as much about Bill as anything.

"Good evening, I'm Bill Hurley," he began as usual. "Before I get to the news I want to wish my bride of thirty years a happy birthday. It's our secret Lila. I won't tell that you were just twenty-two when we married. Anyway, I hope you enjoy my portrait and that you'll hang it in an appropriate place, like over the fireplace. Just kidding. Seriously, it's an Edmund Allbright portrait. He did it for me for free just for mentioning his gallery here on the news.

"Speaking of the news, here is the very latest: police and fire investigators in the San Fernando Valley town of Reseda still aren't saying if a four-alarm blaze early yesterday morning that destroyed most of Virgin Valley Pictures facilities was the work of an arsonist. Fire chief Robert Mason tells KEYT news "Some things suggest arson, but we're not ready to classify it as such just yet." Firefighters battled the blaze for nearly six hours. The film company's main studios, administrative wing and distribution center sustained damages estimated at two-and-a-half million dollars.

"Virgin Valley Pictures is the studio that produced and still distributes *Two on One*, the pornographic film that somehow made it onto the airwaves of this station during our regularly scheduled airing of *The Dodge Dance Party* last Saturday.

"Asked if there was any link between the fire and *The Dodge Dance Party* incident, Reseda Police Chief Nolan Richter said his investigators were exploring it. Hurley paused for effect. "I'll bet the chief's men are fighting over who gets to inspect what's left of all those naughty films."

CHAPTER 12

I t took Reno Parris twelve hours to reach Santa Barbara in the Tacoma, thanks in large part to a leaky water hose. He was lucky to find a repair shop just outside San Luis Obispo. The minute he finally arrived in Santa Barbara he registered at the Sea Breeze.

His first piece of business was to check the phone book on the slight chance he'd find Holly Murchison listed. He'd looked her up on Facebook but her profile provided zero information.

He'd figured Holly for married after all these years, but drew hope from the fact she'd used her maiden name to sign up for the reunion. He was surprised to find her listed. He called first thing.

"It's your long lost lover," Parris began.

"Oh, my God," Holly said, a smile coming through her voice. "You aren't lost Reno, I dumped you, remember?"

Encouraged by the fun reception he'd received, Reno arranged to meet Holly for a drink a half-hour before the reunion. He picked the Double Play, a sports bar just a couple of blocks from the Sea Breeze.

Like the lead in a Spaghetti Western, Reno sauntered through the Double Play's dining room, refusing to acknowledge the other customers. It was his barroom trademark. When he reached the bar he nonchalantly pulled up a stool and placed his black cowboy hat on the counter. "Dewars/rocks by the handful," he said to the bartender. He drained a pair before the bartender could ring him up. Scotch settled his nerves. He realized he was shaky about seeing Holly. If only he didn't have such a big gut. He could kick himself for not staying in shape. He made himself a promise to get back in the gym as soon as he got home. Humping Pearl into the wee hours of the morning three to four times a week wasn't cutting it. He had to do more to burn calories.

Years ago Reno's picture had been hanging on more than one of the Double Play's walls. In between tugging at his drinks, Reno scanned the current gallery for those photos. Nothing. Finally, he asked the bartender.

"You an ex-big leaguer?" the bartender said in a husky, chain-smoker's voice.

"Never made the show, but – "

" Ain't in here, then. Only big timers on these walls." The bartender leaned into Reno's chest and lowered his voice. "If you check the men's room you'll find photos of a couple of porn stars who once frequented this place, but other than that it's all big leaguers. Maybe an ex-NFL guy or two."

Reno didn't have the opportunity to get depressed at being dismissed from the gallery of stars because suddenly there was a hand massaging his shoulder. Instinctively, he inhaled what remained of a third Dewars/rocks and slowly turned around to find Holly Murchison standing before him. Her swimming pool blue eyes twinkled and her "before collagen" full lips shifted up on one side to form her characteristic terminally seductive smile.

"So, why did you break up with me?" Reno said, hopping off his bar stool and greeting Holly with a bear hug.

"Still the same Reno," Holly laughed. "Patience of a saint."

Reno smiled and took her hand. "Join me in sin and misery?"

"Why not?" Holly asked for a vodka martini then placed her suede coat on the back of her stool.

"Fat fuck, aren't I, Holly?"

"Boy you cut right to the chase, Reno. I've forgotten how tasteful you can be. Next, you'll want to know if I'm sleeping with anyone."

"Are you?"

"Jeez."

"Okay, I'll back off." Reno said. "How was your summer vacation?"

"Always trying to push a button, aren't you. For the record, I have someone I sleep with on occasion."

"Like holidays?"

"You're hopeless.

"Who is he?

"Name's Shannon.

"Irish?"

"Last name's Taylor.

"White?"

"Oh, you're wicked."

"He runs a nursery. He's a nice man."

"Is he coming to the reunion?"

"No. He said the night was for taking down demons. He'd rather take out books from the library. He's a voracious reader."

"Sounds like my kinda guy."

"He's as much like you as Pink is Martha Stewart."

"Seriously," Reno said placing his hand over Holly's. "How's your life?"

"Interesting. Yours?"

"Sucks."

"Well, that covers it. It's been a slice, Reno." Holly saluted him with her drink and then pretended to get up from her seat.

"Don't you dare leave me again so soon."

"Beg me to stay. I didn't get the satisfaction last time." Holly gave him an air kiss.

Engrossed as he was in the verbal sparring with Holly, Reno was equally busy sizing her up. He gave her good marks. She was a little worn around the edges – lines around the neck – but in general, he wouldn't hesitate to ride the pony again. Her auburn hair was nearly all gray. It made her look mature, not old. Holly had the Dorothy Hamill look before Dorothy ever laced up skates. Under the black lace shawl she wore over her shoulders, Holly appeared surprisingly fit in an understated black evening dress.

Over another round of drinks they shared the Cliff Notes versions of their lives. Reno wasn't surprised to learn Holly never made it into Berkeley.

"When I got there they said my application had been sent to admissions for review and the next day it was rejected because of 'extenuating circumstances.' I was devastated. I got in touch with others from our class. The same thing

60

had happened to them at UC schools up and down the state. The skin flick, I figured. Thank you Mrs. Pendleton."

"They never even contacted me," Reno said with a look of hurt.

"Hah," Holly laughed. "You couldn't have gotten into the UC system with a hand grenade, Reno. Not with your GPA."

"Ooh!" Reno said with a wince.

Holly asked the bartender for a refill. "So, I turned away from school, I crossed the bay to San Francisco, and like many confused teens, settled in the Haight and became a hippie. I smoked pot, experimented with LSD, demonstrated against the war, fucked a million guys I can't even remember in the name of free love, and tried to commit suicide."

"How?"

"Downers. I forget the pharmaceutical name. I hit bottom in the summer of '69. And then, I became a nun." Holly smiled. "End of story."

"Wow! You fell off 'the most likely to succeed' track early, girl."

"Try not to sugar coat it, Reno."

"Do you think it was the curse?"

"It's why the gang's all here tonight, isn't it?"

"That deserves another drink. In?"

"I usually only have one drink at a time, but what the heck, seeing as how I'm going to have to tell my story more than once tonight."

"But your name is in the phone book. Shouldn't you be in a nuns' home or something?"

"Convent?"

"Took the word right out of my mouth."

"I quit. Just last year."

"I didn't know you could quit God," Reno said.

"I couldn't justify the churches sex scandal cover-ups. The only ones in need of confession were priests."

Reno laughed before he spoke. "Heard the one about the priest who was asked how difficult it was to practice celibacy?"

"I thought I'd heard them all, but no."

"It's child's play, the priest answered."

Holly smiled. "I felt dirty being Catholic. Plus, I'm almost sixty-seven. I've worked hard for a long time. Now I've got a studio on the Mesa. I work a few hours in Shannon's nursery down the street from me and I'm learning to make greeting cards with Photoshop. It's a quiet life, but I have no complaints."

"It's not how I pictured you."

"Enough about me," Holly said. "Your turn, mister baseball."

Reno didn't leave out any of the ugly details. At one point, strangers at the bar began to gather around him.

When he finished Holly placed her hand on his shoulder and smiled. "You're life plays like a twenty car pile-up, Reno."

"Pretty much. But, I'm still stepping up to the plate."

"You always were a scrapper."

Again, Reno placed his hand over Holly's. "We could blow some minds if we walk in together tonight. What do you say?"

Holly smiled. "I'm actually up for it. I haven't acted like a teenager in years. I miss it."

Before opening the front door on their way out of the Double Play, Reno stopped and faced Holly. "Seriously, why did you dump me for Chrissakes?" He put his cowboy hat back on.

"Because I found out about you and Penny Sexton at the drive in."

"Shit! That happened months before. It was before fucking homecoming." Reno put his hand to his mouth. "Sorry, I forget you were a woman of the cloth."

"Took me that long to convince myself that you were a cheater. Plus, I knew you wouldn't take it well."

Reno's smile disappeared. He banged his fist against the jukebox. "I didn't fucking take it well. And fuck it if my language bothers you." He could feel his neck getting hot and the muscles in his face tightening. He was aware that Holly had taken a step back from him. "I swear I can't decide what messed up my life more; being in the class of '62 or getting 86'd by you and your gutless postcard." Reno inhaled deeply, his chest blowing up like a balloon. But he surprised even himself by suddenly breaking out in a big horselaugh. "Just had to get that off my chest," he said. "I apologize."

"It must have weighed heavy on you, Reno."

"Yeah."

"Guess you let your body get bigger for support, huh?"

"Ooh!" Reno feigned taking a knife to his heart. "It's okay for me to call myself a fat ass, but when you do, it hurts."

"Let's go," Holly said, tugging at his elbows. "We have so many more insults to share with one another."

"But you haven't answered my other question," Reno said as the two of them marched arm-in-arm across the gravel parking lot to his truck.

"Which one's that? I only remember the dumping question."

"The one I haven't asked yet," Reno grinned. "What are the chances of the two of us...you know?"

"Good, once hell freezes – "

"Okay, okay. I don't need more rejection in my life. Pretend I never asked."

Holly dropped her head and then smiled.

"But think about it anyway, Sister."

CHAPTER 13

The first thing Dee Dee Wellborn noticed about the person entering the activity room was his suit. She immediately figured him for Whitney Crawford. In all of her emails to classmates she'd urged them to come casual. She was surprised to see anyone arrive so early. The musicians hadn't even begun to set up.

"Where's the registration table?" Whitney asked without saying hello.

"There's no registration. No name tags either. It's not like I'm on a huge budget. I'm Dee Dee Wellborn," she said, offering her hand. "I'm guessing you're Whitney Crawford. Right?"

"That's correct."

Could the guy be more of a stiff, Dee Dee wondered? She wasn't about to tell him she recognized him from his stupid TV commercial. She got embarrassed for him every time she saw it, and it aired daily.

"My competitors call me an ambulance chaser…better than chasing women. If you're looking for a personal injury attorney who is there when you need him...look no further..."

Dee Dee couldn't help notice the manila folder Whitney was carrying under his arm. It was stuffed with papers. She wondered if he'd brought some work along to review in case he ran out things to say to his classmates. "Filing a brief on Monday, Whitney?"

"Hardly," Whitney said with the cold stare of a dead tropical fish. "They're ballots." He made a move to place his folder on a small card table.

Dee Dee abruptly blocked his path. "Last time I looked the evening's agenda didn't call for a vote on anything." Dee Dee's expression read "I'm from cellblock D, don't fuck with me."

"You didn't get my email?" Whitney fooled with his tie.

"I don't get you. What are we voting on?"

"Who did it."

Dee Dee scowled at the remark. "Who did what?"

Whitney backed up a step and swallowed heavily. "Who put the *skin flick* on the air in 1962 in the middle of *The Dodge Dance Party*?"

" Great," Dee Dee said. "Growing up here I always figured the Sea Breeze for a great place to hold a trial."

"It works for me." Whitney said, setting up a table for his ballots.

Dee Dee placed her hand on her stomach as if to stop a laugh. She failed, however. The laugh was so loud and long she needed a tissue to stop her eyes from tearing. "So, we mark our ballots and then take the winner, or loser in this case, out to the parking lot and slap jumper cables to his testicles and then call in the cops?

"Who says it was a he?"

"Point well taken, counselor."

"Thank you."

Whitney stepped around Dee Dee and placed his folder on the table. "I've got five nominees on each ballot."

"And how did you arrive at the names of the nominees?"

"Common sense: reputations, circumstances. Trust me. I'm on target." What Whitney failed to tell Dee Dee was his plan to cross-examine the top three vote getters in front of all of their classmates. He was convinced he could extract the identity of the true culprit through his line of questioning.

"And when does the judge show up?"

"We're the judge."

"What kind of sentence does this verdict carry?"

"Scorn."

"Jesus Christ," Dee Dee said, suddenly aware that people were beginning to arrive in the parking lot. "This great search for the truth is pro bono no doubt." Dee Dee shook her head. "If he played the flick, you must not acquit."

Dee Dee reached for Whitney's folder, but stopped short of taking it. "This is just crazy enough that it might be more entertaining than the music."

"You said in your emails you wanted cleansing."

Dee Dee placed her hands on her hips and looked squarely into Whitney's tiny eyes. "I would have been better off booking Mr. Clean."

CHAPTER 14

Nearly a month after the public airing of the *skin flick* the County coroner determined that Orrin Burdette had died from a heart attack. Edna Pendleton Wright's public outrage during that time had noticeably exceeded any public display of remorse for her fallen chief engineer. The Santa Barbara News Press ran a front-page story on Orrin Burdette's funeral and devoted special attention to the fact Mrs. Pendleton Wright was not in attendance.

In a paid newspaper ad, however, Edna attacked school administrators, school board trustees and the parents of San Marcos' graduating class for exhibiting irresponsible leadership and guidance. She also chided the police for failing to make an arrest. During an extended prime time interview with one of her own TV news reporters on her own station she called the *dirty movie* "the most vile act imaginable." She called it a pockmark on the city's storied history.

In the fallout, Chief McWorter, who'd been on the city's police force for twenty-five years, the last seven as chief, was fired. City manager Marshall Hambrick, acting on the recommendation of the city council, cited perform-ance issues as the reason for the chief's dismissal. Bottom line – he'd come up empty in the *skin flick* investigation. All he'd been able to verify was that there had been no forced entry into master control. There were no witnesses, no prints, no nothing.

City council member Ian Webster was the chief''s most outspoken opponent. Webster, who is a member of a com-munity council that advises KEYT's management on local programming, called the incident "Santa Barbara's darkest hour", and was on record blaming Chief McWorter for not devoting sufficient resourses to the investigation and for failing to demonstrate proper discretion in the raid on the Coral Casino.

Chief McWorter didn't go down quietly. In a radio interview on KIST, he blamed his ouster on "influence pedaling" by Edna Pendleton Wright. "Judge Garland acted as her point man," he told the interviewer. "He went to the each member of the city council with an ultimatum: get rid of me or forget Mrs. Wright's ten-million dollar gift to the renovation of the Performing Arts Center."

The chief didn't stop there. "Judge Garland has a per-sonal vendetta against me because I busted his nephew my first year as chief. Bastard operated one of the most sophis-ticated Ponzi schemes in county history."

In a parting shot at Edna Pendleton Wright, the chief said, "Maybe if she'd aired weekend Dodger games like the ABC affiliate in San Luis Obispo instead of that second rate accordion player with the bubble machine, none of this would have happened."

CHAPTER 15

By her unofficial count, all of Dee Dee Wellborn's classmates who'd RSVP'd showed up, about thirty in all. So too had a dozen or so League of Women Voters members carrying protest signs outside the entrance to the activity center that read, "Class of '62, Still Dirty Words." The grads attending represented less than five percent of the senior class, but when Dee Dee had first decided to pursue a reunion she'd have settled for ten people. Spouses and dates pushed the total attendance to around forty-five. The Sea Breeze's activity center was at or above capacity. From time to time Anthony Castello would pop in and take his own count. He explained to Dee Dee that he didn't want to give the police another excuse to raid the place.

Dee Dee wasn't surprised that the early activity took place at the bar. Reno Parris was the catalyst. After he and Holly had in fact turned heads with their entrance, Reno sprinted to the bar where he ordered Skip and Go Nakeds – gin, sweet and sour, and beer– for the first dozen class members to join him. "To Lawrence Welk and his fabulous champagne music makers," Reno said, raising his glass toward the ceiling. "Now lets fry the asshole responsible for all our suffering."

"Here, here," someone shouted.

After Holly whispered something his ear, Reno threw up his hands in an appeal for quiet. "Less we forget him, I suggest we set up a college scholarship fund for a San Marcos senior in Orrin Burdette's name. I'm willing to bet Dee Dee will take your checks. Reno conducted a brief check of the contents of his wallet. "Hell, I'm in for a hundred,"

There was enthusiastic applause from every corner of the activity center.

"Finally," someone in the back of the activity room shouted. "Only fifty years in the making."

There was a smattering of laughter from the gathered.

The musicians started playing earlier than Dee Dee had requested, which worried her that they might ask for more than the seventy-five dollars they'd agreed upon. They called themselves *The Occasions*. Their promotional material, which consisted of handwritten Post-Its with a phone number, stressed there was no occasion they wouldn't play for, including pet memorials. They were the only ones within twenty-five square-miles of Santa Barbara who Dee Dee could find to perform for the class of '62. *The Occasions*— a guy on keyboard, a bass player, a drummer and a female vocalist who doubled on bass guitar – were all in their late twenties. Their music was Steely Dan on anti-depressants.

Outside of Reno and Holly masquerading as a couple, Linda Dalby and her date, Scott Clayton, generated the biggest buzz. Scott was Zeke Clayton's son, which immediately elevated him to celebrity status.

Linda Dalby was elegantly dressed in a black, sleeveless Christian Dior dress. Her blonde hair pulled back in a bun, she appeared fit and fresh and as much as ten years younger than any of her female classmates.

"Either the years have been kind to her or she's found the Mercedes of face doctors," Reno said to more than one person.

Linda had been at the top of nearly every boy's *A* list in high school. She had the legs of a Go Go dancer, a dynamite personality and a reputation as the best French kisser this side of Leslie Caron. She dated mostly college guys, however, because, as she put it, "The only time a high school boy has an original thought is in a wet dream."

Linda made no secret of her aspiration to jump straight from homecoming queen to Hollywood starlet. A year out of high school she landed a small part in The Fugitive TV series as Lieutenant Girard's desk assistant, but that was it. She surprised even herself by placing her career on hold to marry a record company executive who got his feet put to the fire in the Payola scandal and spent seven years in prison. She divorced him the day after he was released from San Quentin and re-married a month later. She had three kids with her second husband, an accountant for Universal Studios, who up and left her after twelve years for a former UCLA fraternity brother.

About the time the last of her kids left home for college, Linda had a spiritual awakening. She became a Buddhist and subsequently took a job as a tour guide for the New Dawn Center in Sedona, Arizona. She was in charge of shuttling participants in the Center's Soul Enhancement Workshops back and forth from L.A. every weekend. The shuttle is how she recently met Scott Clayton. He'd booked the Center's workshop as a last ditch effort to find the inner peace he'd been seeking for more years than he could count. They happened to sit next to one another on the bus ride to Sedona and, although Linda was almost twice his age, they became fast friends; meeting and talking during most of the workshops break periods and meals. In a matter of a single weekend, Linda returned to her roots and became a spiritual cheerleader for Scott.

Scott was the only child born to Zeke and Alesandra Carmen-Meza, an Argentine novella star. They divorced when he was three and because they were both deep into their careers, Scott was shipped off to Santa Barbara to live with his grandparents. Howard and Margaret Clayton raised him until he was eighteen and joined the Army. Once he finished his military obligation, Scott set out to become an actor. At twenty-five, he was handed star billing in two of his dad's films. Despite being Hollywood handsome – tall, dark and athletic with abs that could bounce coins – Scott didn't sell. He played action heroes in both films, but lacked charisma. "His performance was as flat as a movie screen that's been run over by an eighteen wheeler," the L.A. Times movie critic wrote in his review of *Dead Man's Crossing*. Both of Scott's films were box office busts. Shortly after, Daddy Zeke cut his ties both professionally and personally. For the next five years Scott didn't do much but cocaine and drag his dad's name through the tabloids with such scandalous behavior that *The Hollywood Reporter* joked, "Zeke Clayton needs to get a restraining order against his son's reputation."

Scott hit bottom when he nearly drowned trying to surf Rincon during a weeklong drug and alcohol binge.

"He's such a package, girlfriend," a voice whispered in Linda Dalby's ear. "Can you handle him at your age?"

"Girl, how are you?" Linda said, embracing a smiling Penny Sexton, her strawberry hair of forty years now a deep rust color.

"Surviving the curse. It's what I do best. And you?"

"Same," Linda said.

"God, I never thought I'd be waiting tables at fifty years after graduating high school, but that time is near." Penny shrugged her shoulders then threw down the remainder of her gin and tonic. "Buy you a drink, Linda?"

"No thanks, Penny. My highs are strictly spiritual now."

"That's not the homecoming queen I knew and loathed," Penny laughed.

Linda dismissed the comment. "Who are you with?" she said.

"The hand." Penny raised her right hand.

Linda's eyebrows lifted. "Is that a joke?"

"No. It's all I need anymore. It gives me an orgasm without the grief. Don't have to cook for it, wash for it, sew for it, wait up nights for it or suck its dick."

Linda forced a smile that didn't work. Searching for an escape, she glanced in Scott's direction. He was talking with Reno at the bar. "I'll catch up with you later, Penny, my date is keeping the wrong company," she said.

Penny shot her eyes in Reno's direction. "That bastard is the last person I hoped would be here tonight."

"I'm floored by how well you continue to this day to conceal your feelings about him, Penny."

CHAPTER 16

What pleased Dee Dee even more than the good turnout was the surprise appearance of her new interest, Mustafa Muhammad – M&M, as he likes to be called. He'd told her he would be out of town on business the night of the reunion, recruiting investors for a chain of Tae Kwan Do studios. Mustafa, who for the first forty years of his life went by the name Rodney Rodgers, met Dee Dee online – a singles site. He'd listed his preferences in women as:

"Mature. Intelligent. Independent. Full Figured. White."

Under the heading of "own best qualities," he wrote: "Ability to please partner –sexually, spiritually, socially."

"Imagine," she'd said to herself countless times, "someone willing to please me." Dee Dee would have been down right ecstatic if he'd included financially. "This close to the grand slam," she told a friend.

Given her age and her recent experience with an AARP Gold Card member who had a caboose that resembled a waffle iron, Dee Dee was giddy about attracting a man with a tight ass. He could have had a middle eye as long as his bupkus was tight. She viewed a possible relationship with Mustafa as risk free even if he turned out to be a serial killer. What did she have to lose, her reputation?

"You could get lucky tonight," Dee Dee said as she greeted Mustafa with a big smile and an embrace that looked as if it could have hurt. "Thank you for coming. Now I won't have to hustle the drummer. He's cute but he has no ass. Pants barely stay above his crack.

Mustafa, who was dressed in a lemon-lime Kaftan and fashioned dirty brown dreadlocks, smiled. "I'm here to serve." He placed his arm around Dee Dee's ample waist and at the same time, after checking to see if anyone was looking, took her hand and nonchalantly guided it over his fully involved package. "Care to dance?" he said.

"Is that your best offer?"

"Just my initial one, sweet thing."

Dee Dee pressed hard against her new man and began swaying to the music that vaguely reminded her of *Rikki Don't Lose That Number* in slow play.

As happy as Dee Dee was with the way the reunion was unfolding, she confided in Mustafa that she wished Whitney Crawford hadn't come. Who could blame her? Every fifteen minutes Whitney would commandeer the microphone from The Occasions' vocalist and announce time was running out for people to cast their ballots. "Help me find the truth, brothers and sisters."

Just as the music stopped for what The Occasions vocalist announced would be their first break of the evening, Dee Dee felt her cell phone vibrate against her hip. Before she'd lost weight she missed several calls a week.

"Lance Vance, here. Channel Three Action News," a voice greeted her.

"I'm not inclined to take your call," Dee Dee said, slapping the cell unit closed. Prior to the reunion Dee Dee had notified the News Press, Channel Three and the two radio stations that carried local news that they wouldn't be welcome at the Sea Breeze.

Her cell vibrated again. "What don't you understand about not being welcome?" she said.

This time Lance Vance was more assertive, informing Dee Dee that he and his crew would be at the Sea Breeze to do a live hit for the eleven o'clock news. Dee Dee threatened to call police if he showed.

"Do you honestly think Chief Franklin McWorter, Jr." he emphasized the word junior, "would offer assistance to anyone from the class of '62?" Vance's laughed. "If a guy with a pipe bomb phoned in a threat to your party the chief would make sure the caller had Mapquest directions."

Dee Dee was told she could expect the Action News crew to begin doing interviews and setting up for a live hit within the hour. She was advised to clear space in the parking lot for the station's microwave truck.

"Fuck!" she said, ramming her cell back into its holster.

"Now?" Mustafa said.

Dee Dee's eyebrows lifted. "That's an idea," she smiled, her eyes suddenly flashing. "The manager offered me his only suite in case I needed to stash party drunks."

"I'm starting to feel nauseous and very unsteady," Mustafa said with a grin.

Dee Dee took Mustafa by the hand and together they marched in the direction of the rear exit. She adjusted their route as she approached the finger food table in order to speak to Whitney Crawford. "Don't announce the voting results until I get back."

"How long will it be?" Whitney said, his eyebrows pinching above his nose.

"How long will it be, babe?" Dee Dee said looking into Mustafa's eyes.

"Close to eleven inches."

Dee Dee wore a look of pride.

Whitney stared blankly at the two of them.

CHAPTER 17

I t wasn't until news of Chief McWorter's firing had spread throughout the community that Whitney Crawford learned he'd been the only student arrested in the Coral Casino raid. It made him furious to think that Reno Parris (notorious prankster), Vaughn Berglund (audio-visual guy), Wayne Preston (cousin in porn films) and Edgar Peoples (school's only black) weren't jailed as well.

Initially, Whitney was placed in the drunk tank; a single cell infested with winos, dope addicts, sexual deviants and drugstore robbers. Victoria, a 6'-2" black transvestite with arms the size of baby redwoods, was the first to approach Whitney, who had buried his head against the concrete wall at the end of the cell's only bench.

"Darlin' what's a virgin like you doin' in a place like this?"

Whitney didn't answer.

"Cat got your tongue, darlin'?"

Whitney shrugged off her long violet nails the second the touched his shoulder, but he said nothing.

"That's a cryin' shame, darlin' because I was doin' some serious hopin' that you could use that tongue to lick my organ until my black ass turns white."

Whitney sat up quickly. His face was flushed; his eyes were rolled back. In an instant he pitched his head forward and chucked his mother's meat loaf all over Victoria's black patent leather spiked heels.

"Punk ass, sissy, white trash," Victoria said, adjusting the waist of her pink A-line skirt.

Shortly after midnight Whitney was transferred to a small, sterile looking room on the second floor of the jail. Chief McWorter assumed the role of lead interrogator. Two uniformed sergeants stood watch.

"Just tell me how you did it, son and I'll make it easier on you," McWorter said. He was hunched over a gray Formica table, his arms extended for support. His eyes never left his young suspect. "What was your weapon of choice?"

"I didn't do it," Whitney said, too soft for the chief's liking.

"Speak up for Chrissakes. You've got balls and a sack, don't you?"

"Yes," Whitney said, louder this time.

Chief McWorter started pacing in front of the room's two-way mirror. "Do you have someone who can speak for your whereabouts between the hours of 9:00PM and 9:30PM this evening?"

"Last night," the sergeant said. "For the record, Chief."

"My mother," Whitney said. "She was making rhubarb pie in the kitchen."

"Did she see you during that time?"

"Yes."

"Can you elaborate?"

Whitney's face turned ghostly white. He swallowed heavily.

"I don't have all night," the chief said, again leaning on the big table with his elbows.

"Morning, Chief," the same sergeant corrected him.

The chief moved again. This time he crouched in front of Whitney and pushed his face to within an inch of the boy's nose. Whitney could smell garlic on his breath. "At this very moment son you are in desperate need of a corroborating witness. Now, exactly where did your mother see you?"

Whitney inhaled deeply and placed his hand to his forehead. "The bathroom, sir."

"Go on."

"Ah...I had...ah...been in my bedroom for several hours and – "

"Get to the point, son"

Whitney's whole body hiccupped. "She came to check on me and when I wasn't there, she looked in the bathroom." Tears started to well in Whitney's eyes. "I...ah...I thought I'd locked the door. When she came in – "

"Don't tell me she caught you jerking your monkey?"

Whitney began to bawl.

Chief McWorter moved toward the door. "See if his mother has the same story, sergeant. If she does, release the boy before someone in Block B yanks his carrot for him."

CHAPTER 18

Out-of-towners like Reno Parris, Linda Dalby, and Wayne Preston dropped their collective jaws when Vaughn Berglund's male nurse wheeled him into the Sea Breeze activity center. Vaughn was slumped in his wheelchair, his head to one side, his eyes fixed on the floor. There was nothing about him that suggested he knew where he was.

Those who'd never left Santa Barbara after high school, like Dee Dee Wellborn —except for ten years in the slammer —Whitney Crawford, Edgar Peoples and Penny Sexton, already knew Vaughn's story, having run across the shell of a man around town at least once in fifty years. Among the locals he was the unofficial poster boy of the curse.

Vaughn, who still wore his sandy hair in Art Garfunkle fashion, was the only San Marcos grad from the class of '62 to make it into a state run university – UC Davis with an interest in veterinary medicine. Vaughn's father, a highly respected cancer researcher, had once roomed with the UC vice-chancellor as an undergraduate at Stanford.

By his junior year, Vaughn, a strong voice among anti-war activists, began dropping acid like it was candy. One night at an SDS sponsored membership-recruiting party he got hold of some bad stuff. His brain fried before he could receive medical attention.

Out-of-towners and locals were surprised to find Vaughn's name on Whitney's "Who Did It" ballot.

"How's he going to defend himself?" one alum wondered aloud.

"Even if he did it," Linda Dalby said, "he's paid for it ten times over."

"I can't believe he's even here," Bonnie Lovell said.

"I hear it was his sister's idea," Brian said. "She supervises him now that the parents are dead. Probably figures any social stimulus is a plus."

Vaughn's name was listed alongside Reno Parris, Wayne Preston, Penny Sexton and Gil Sandoval, a counselor, whose brother was a film director. Edgar People's name was originally on Whitney's ballot but when he found out about it he went ballistic, threatening Whitney with legal action if he didn't exclude him from the candidates.

"This is racially motivated," Edgar had screamed at Whitney as many of the guests were arriving. Dressed in a burgundy leather jumpsuit that could suffocate a lesser man and flashing a gold chain big enough to anchor the Queen Mary, Edgar could have easily been confused for the evening's entertainment. "Affirmative action does not apply to law and order," he ranted. "Not on this nigger's watch. How can we rid ourselves of the curse, when this guy's allowed to work the house," Edgar said, repeatedly jabbing his index finger at Whitney.

Whitney had to take a black Sharpie to Edgar's name on each of the ballots. Edgar watched from over Whitney's shoulder to make sure he didn't miss a single one.

It had been close to a half-hour by Whitney's count since Dee Dee and Mustafa had left the party. The instant Whitney saw her return, hopelessly trying to re-shape her damaged spike job and walking gingerly, he hopped on the stage, nudged the female vocalist with his elbow and grabbed the microphone from its stand.

"Fellow class members, may I have your attention?" A drum roll followed. Whitney didn't care for the sound effects, motioning for the musicians to leave the stage.

Slowly, the majority of class members, most with drinks firmly in hand and buzzes kicking in, began gathering around Whitney.

"I applaud your diligence," Whitney said without any expression. "Thirty ballots were printed and they've all been filled out and returned. Clearly, you have chosen this occasion to be responsible adults."

Reno's voice boomed from the area of bar. "If you ain't a responsible adult by now, you'd better not take a test drive tonight cause you're liable to discover it's not worth the trouble."

"Thanks for that observation, Parris," Whitney said with a deep sigh.

Wayne Preston couldn't resist an opportunity. "Only thing you're responsible for Reno is a miserable .226 lifetime batting average."

Everyone roared except Whitney. He played with the knot in his tie as he waited for silence. "Can we limit the extraneous comments?" he said, his narrow eyes scanning the room. "I only have so much time for this."

Whitney paused to shuffle notes he'd made. "I've counted all the ballots and here are the results."

The room suddenly became quiet.

Whitney cleared his throat. "The person the majority of you think did it…with a total of seventeen votes is…"

Collectively, those representing the class of '62 inhaled.

"Vaughn Berglund," Whitney said, his voice louder than it had been.

In unison, class members gasped. It sounded like thirty people had just pulled alongside a five-car crash. Vaughn's nurse began to cry. "Shameful," his lips read.

Whitney sensed the potential for outrage. He pushed on with his agenda. "Next, with nine votes; Reno Parris."

Reno tipped his cowboy hat. "More than happy to be playin' second fiddle to – "

"And in third place with four votes," Whitney said, his face still without expression, "Penny Sexton."

Penny's face turned as red as a summer sunset. "F-all of you," she hissed, spinning on her heels and heading for the entrance.

"Don't go far, Sexton," Whitney said. "You'll have a chance to defend yourself when I cross-examine you. I promise."

Dee Dee's antenna sparked like it was the 4th of July. What the hell was he talking about, she wondered? Was the little fuck really planning a trial in the middle of her party? She approached the stage at a jog. She wore a prison look: nostrils flared, eyes glazed, and teeth clenched. "What the hell are you doing?"

"I'm going to cross-examine the top three vote getters." Whitney stepped back as if he was expecting Dee Dee to become physical.

"On my death," Dee Dee's face turned blistery red. She stood braced in front of Whitney – legs spread, hands on hips.

"How else are we going to find out who did it?" Whitney said softly.

"We're here to lift a curse, not convict," Dee Dee said between clinched teeth. "Listen you little shitbag, after seeing how the voting affected Penny, I'm not letting you – "

Someone at a distance with a deep, powerful voice interrupted. "I'm looking for a Dee Dee Wellborn."

Dee Dee turned to find a tall, blonde, man standing at the entrance to the activity center. He wore a powder blue Action News blazer with a big number three emblazoned on his lapel. Next to him, a shabbily dressed younger man carried a video camera on his shoulder and a handful of portable lights.

"I'm who you're looking for," Dee Dee said. "Didn't your mother tell you it isn't polite to interrupt?"

"Lance Vance, here. Where's the best place for us to set up?" he said. "I want to interview some of the guests."

"I want a houseboat on Lake Cachuma," Dee Dee said. "Why don't we step outside and discuss why you and your shaggy dog sidekick aren't going to play TV here tonight?" Dee Dee made her way through those who were still gathered around the stage and approached Lance. She grabbed him by the elbow and spun him in the direction of the door. "Let's go," she said.

Reno shouted from the bar, "Here's twenty bucks on Dee Dee by TKO."

Desperately in need of an endorsement for his agenda, Whitney asked for the laughing to stop. "Let's all vote," he said. "How many object to me interrogating our top three vote getters?"

There was no response: just lots of blank faces.

"I'm in," Reno shouted, breaking the awkward silence. "I'll let you question me until your throat runs dry. Besides this big gut of mine, I got nothing to hide."

A couple people clapped.

Whitney asked everyone to grab a folding chair from the closet and form a circle in the middle of the room. He smiled for the first time. He appeared energized by Reno's response. "I want two chairs in the middle, facing each other. I want to be able to look the person I'm interrogating in the eyes.

"Do they have to look into your beady eyes?" someone shouted.

At this point, more than likely under Dee Dee's direction, three members of the catering staff began circulating with large plates of hors de oeuvres.

Whitney was too focused on the task at hand to be bothered by the activity. He placed his chair in the center of the circle and doodled on a legal pad as he waited for his classmates to get their food and settle. A majority of them stopped at the bar for refills. Whitney checked the entrance repeatedly for any sign of Dee Dee.

"Are we ready to roll, counselor?" Reno said, taking his seat like he'd mount a horse.

"Just waiting for your classmates full attention, Parris."

"*Silencio, por favor!*" Reno shouted, holding up the palms of his hands. "I want to have time for last call in case I'm found guilty."

More clapping.

Whitney began by asking Reno to state his name and address.

"No fuckin' way you're getting my address, pal. Next thing I know the IRS is camped at my door like a lost puppy." Reno shifted in his chair, amused by his own clever self.

"In the interest of maintaining a professional decorum I must insist you refer to me as Mr. Crawford."

"Okay, Whitney," Reno said with a grin as big as his belly.

Whitney checked the activity center entrance again before launching his questioning. "Can you establish your whereabouts, Parris, on the evening of June 19th, 1962?"

"Sure, Whitney. I was at the senior party, like everyone else." Reno paused for effect. "Come to think of it counselor, I didn't see you there."

"This isn't about me. Please edit your remarks, Parris."

"I just want all the truths about that night out in the open, Whitney."

"I'm sure your classmates appreciate you being so conscientious, Parris." Whitney got out of his chair and began pacing the inner portion of the circle. He no longer looked at Reno as he spoke, choosing instead to stare off at the ceiling. "The party didn't begin until 8:30PM. Where were you between the hours of 6:00PM and 8:30PM?"

Reno placed his hand to his chin. "6:00PM to 7:30PM I had a few beers in the parking lot at Henry's Beach. Couple of guys from the baseball team wanted to reminisce. After that —"

"Where did you get the beer?"

Reno pivoted in his seat in order to track Whitney's movement. "That would be implementing someone."

"Implicating," Whitney said with a sigh. "How'd you every pass Miss Burke's English class, anyway?"

"Whatever," Reno said with a shrug of his shoulders.

"Let's return to your timeline, Parris. What did you do after you finished having beers with your buddies?"

"That gets kinda personal."

"Please answer the question."

"I drove back to the house...ah...actually, I stopped at the drug store first. Brown's Pharmacy on State."

"And?"

"I picked up some supplies."

"For what?"

Penny Sexton, who'd returned to the party only moments prior, giggled out loud. Whitney pressed on. "Can you be specific?"

"Jeez. I gotta spell it out for you, Whitney?"

"Yes."

Reno rolled his eyes. "Holly's a pretty girl, right? Was then, still is." Reno searched out Holly in the crowd for her reaction. He was pleased that she was smiling.

"I'm not here to make value judgments," Whitney snapped.

"Take my word for it then, counselor."

"So noted."

"We'd been going steady for almost three years and never once...you know –"

"Huh!" Penny blurted out. "And it never rains in Southern California."

Reno did his best to ignore Penny. "I figured since it was our last school dance and all, I'd be horny as the Devil...and, maybe, you know, I should take some precautions. Know what I'm saying?"

"Specifiy, Parris."

"For Chrissakes, man. I bought some rubbers."

Laughter swept the room. Both Reno and Holly enjoyed the moment. Wayne Preston got up from his chair, walked over to Reno and "high-fived" him.

Whitney used the interruption to sit back down and review some notes. "And after that you went home to dress for the party?" he finally said.

"Why are you asking me if you already know the answer?"

Whitney ignored the question. "Is there anyone who can place you at your house around that time?"

"Holly. Her mother dropped her off at my house after I'd called to say I was running late."

Before Whitney could call on her, Holly stood up and vouched for Reno. "I remember being mad at him for having liquor on his breath in front of my mom."

For whatever reasons, a few in the audience got out of their chairs and migrated toward the bar. Whitney didn't notice them. He plodded forward. "Did you go directly from your house to the Coral Casino, Parris?"

"After Holly and I ...you know, played kissy face in my car."

"Which was –"

"Parked in her driveway. "Man if you'd seen the low cut dress she was wearing you'd understand. Anyway, we got to the party about a half hour late."

"At approximately 9:15PM, some fifteen minutes after you arrived, something out of the ordinary happened that anyone present would remember. Can you tell me what it was?"

Reno slapped his hand against his thigh and laughed. "You bet. Edgar tried doing the Twist. It was shocking because we all figured black guys naturally have rhythm.

Not our boy, Edgar. He looked like a constipated ostrich trying his damndest to take a shit."

Before the laughter died, Edgar jumped from his seat and pretended to slap Reno's face with the back of his hand. He repeated the action several times. "I want you to know," Edgar said, "I've had a soul transplant since those days." Clearly, Edgar's disposition had improved.

"If you don't mind returning to your seat, people," Whitney said, raising his voice. He then turned back to Reno. "Is that all you recall, Parris? Nothing else surprising happened?"

Reno rolled his eyes upward. "Oh, yeah! I remember. Mickey Benes, Mark Pendry and…can't picture the third guy…they came out dressed in skirts and girl's wigs and pretended to be the Lennon Sisters. They sang acappella. It was outrageous."

"Do you remember what they sang?"

"Ooh!" Reno's eyes searched the ceiling. "Wasn't it Tammy? You know, 'the owl hootie hoots to the …' something or other. 'Tammy's in love.'" Several in the gathering booed Reno's attempt at singing.

Whitney sighed. "Do you recall the color of their outfits?"

"It was God awful," Reno grinned. "Lime green."

Whitney's face suddenly turned gray. He slowly stood up in front of Reno's chair and stared down at the linoleum floor. "You're free to go, Parris. You didn't do it."

Reno jumped up and raised a fist. "Yahoo!" he hollered and then pointed in the direction of the bartender. "Skip and Go Naked's for the house."

Everyone representing the class of '62 stepped lively to the bar. *The Occasions* improvised their way through a hybrid version of *Scotch and Soda*: a little bit Kingston Trio and a little bit Beach Boys.

Whitney shouted above the music and noise, "Vaughn Berglund, is next."

CHAPTER 19

It had been a month since JFK's assassination and Edna Pendleton Wright was still so distressed she considered postponing her wedding. Her family had homes on both Nantucket Island and Martha's Vineyard and her dad was a casual acquaintance of Joseph Kennedy. She worried that celebrating so soon after the assassination would be inappropriate. She wasn't even sure she could enjoy Christmas, having already called off the station's annual holiday party.

The wedding had figured to be Santa Barbara's social event of the year. It wasn't long after the *dirty movie* as Edna continued to call it, that she and Judge Garland became public with their relationship. "He has been my strength," was how Edna responded to any and all direct inquiries as to their social status.

The wedding date wasn't an issue with the judge. He was so busy orchestrating his bride's vendetta against the class of '62 he didn't have time to think about anything else. He grumbled to close friends that he worked harder when he was on the bench. But, he confided to Edna that he was enjoying putting the screws to the young people. "It empowers me," he'd said to Edna. "All those marijuana smoking teenage punks who skated out of my courtroom over the years – I feel like I'm finally getting even. There is justice after all," he was fond of saying. "Winston Garland justice."

What really excited the judge was that he'd recently found a possible way of keeping tabs on the class of '62 for years to come. It was the ultimate surveillance tool. He'd flown to the east coast to meet with an associate of J.C.R. Licklider, a computer researcher at MIT. Licklider was on record as envisioning a globally interconnected set of computers, called a "Galactic Network," through which everyone could quickly access data and programs from any site. The judge was bright enough to see the future. "Soon," he reported back to Edna, "they'll be able to network data. And, when they do we'll be able to track everyone in that class for the rest of their lives. Think of the havoc we can create. There is not one kid from that class that won't spend the better part of his or her life looking over his or her shoulder wondering how did this or that person know that about me?"

"And you were worried how you were going to keep yourself busy in retirement, Winston" was Edna's response to the news.

Even though the private eye she'd hired to track the judge during his trip to Boston reported he'd had a liaison with a "professional" as he put it, Edna was so thrilled by the judge's discovery she convinced him to elope. She liked the idea of having a companion in the chaos she was generating. They were married at The Chapel of Love in Las

Vegas, just a block south of the strip. That night Edna lost her "back-up" cherry to the judge. That's the way she tells it anyway. When they finally untangled from one another just before sunrise, Edna confessed to the judge that she'd been amazingly sexually charged ever since she'd seen that *dirty movie*.

CHAPTER 20

Enjoying a spectacular view of the sun setting on the Pacific from the El Encanto's open-air deck was impossible for Zeke Clayton. His mind was still replaying his misadventure on the 425-yard par four, 15th at Sandpiper. His "latest and greatest" Callaway driver had betrayed him, pushing his tee-shot wide right into a patch of ice plant. Zeke held his temper in check because he believed the errant shot was the result of Don Iverson talking about his San Roque Ranch project in the middle of his backswing, rather than his own bad mechanics. Instead of taking a drop and giving up a stroke, Zeke elected to play his way out. It was the worst decision he'd made since the drive north this morning when he finally had to tell Lonnie to stop humming him before he crashed the Mercedes. When he finally hacked his ball free of the club grabbing ice plant and reached the fairway, Zeke was laying four. His wedge, not surprisingly, wound up lying next to a pile of driftwood on the beach, a good hundred feet below.

To make matters worse, Eldridge Brinkman, the head of the Santa Barbara Film Commission, had crushed his longest drive of the day: 265-yards dead center of the fairway. Zeke could see his two-stroke lead evaporating faster than radiator fluid in the Mojave.

Zeke's strategy for the remainder of the hole was strictly damage control. If he could reach the green from 175 yards, he'd maybe drop only two strokes to Eldridge. He could get those back on the next hole, a treacherous par three over water. Unfortunately, he hit a five-iron fat that dropped forty yards short of the green into a gully full of tall weeds and rocks. "A fucking five stroke swing," he said to Enrique as he tossed down his third vodka rocks in fifteen minutes. "Now, I'm down by three strokes with three to play. And worse, my ass is puckering like it's being held to a fire."

"And you made me promise him a stroke a hole," Enrique said with a grimace.

"I put an end to that after the third hole. I could tell the guy played like his personality; boring but efficient."

"Do I want to know how the last three holes played?"

"They didn't," Zeke said with a sheepish grin.

"You didn't. Not after the incident at Rancho Mirage."

"No, I didn't throw my clubs."

"I'm afraid to hear this, boss."

"I took every last club out of my bag, dumped them on the concrete path and ran over them a half-dozen times with my cart.

Zeke's fourth vodka gimlet ran him past 7:00PM. Enrique reminded him he had a 7:30PM dinner reservation.

"Damn! I almost forgot. The fucking police chief."

"And his homely wife."

"How much shit can one man tolerate in a day?"

"You've got to sweet talk him, boss. You said yourself, Brinkman wouldn't budge, even after you bought him golf and loaded him up on drinks."

"His drink is ice tea. What a sterile sumbitch he is, Enrique."

It took Zeke a half hour to change – twenty minutes to jump Lonnie's bones on the couch and ten to shower and dress – which put him fifteen minutes late for dinner. After introductions he apologized for his tardiness. "I hate it when actors are late getting to the set," Zeke said. "And I hate comparing myself to actors."

The chief was decked out in his dress blues. His brass sparkled, even in a dimly lit dining room. Zeke couldn't believe how much Junior looked like his father, right down to the dimple on his chin. The only difference Zeke could tell between them was Junior had the makings of a beer gut. Zeke remembered his father as being remarkably fit.

Eileen McWorter was as Enrique had suggested, homely, and that was being kind, Zeke thought. She was plump, ivory skinned, and had moles sprinkled about her fat neck. She wore thick glasses and appeared slightly cross-eyed when you looked dead on at her. The Chief must have knocked her up, Zeke concluded. He wondered if they still had sex.

Zeke could tell by the way the chief ogled Lonnie's breasts – some relationships last longer – that he was still capable of lust. Admittedly, Lonnie was an eyeful in a blue Donna Karan evening dress whose neckline plunged so deep it should have come packaged with scuba gear. Her visibly rock hard nipples served as magnets to the chief's eyes.

Worried that Lonnie might, in time, feel like she'd become a museum piece, Zeke ordered a round of drinks.

But before they arrived, he asked if the chief if the two of them could get to business.

"I'm enjoying the company," he said, his eyes shifting between Zeke and Lonnie's breasts. "What's the rush? I promised myself I'd drop by that '62 reunion tonight, but there's plenty of time for that. You know it's tonight, don't you?"

"I've got a man going there." Zeke smiled. "Location research, you know."

"Did you know I still have an open file on that *skin flick* case. Before he died my dad made me promise I'd continue the investigation until I solved the mystery."

Zeke started to drink from his glass and then set it down. "I should incorporate that in the film," he said. "It could make for a powerful scene."

Junior sighed and looked at Eileen. "Unfortunately, you can't make your movie in this town, Clayton."

Zeke stirred the ice in his empty drink with his index finger. "I was hoping you might change your mind once we finally got face-to-face."

"I've played with the numbers a dozen times. We just can't afford the overtime."

"Ooh!" Lonnie squealed. She'd dropped some ice down the front of her dress. Gentlemen that he fancies himself, Zeke quickly wiped down the exposed portions of her wet breasts with his napkin. When he finished he looked back at Junior. His eyes were locked on the action and his mouth was open like a man with a sinus condition, all of which presented Zeke an idea.

"Will you ladies excuse us for a moment?" Zeke said as he stood up from the table.

Junior's eyebrows rose. "Where we going, Clayton?"

"Just a word or two in private if that's okay, chief?"

The chief undid the napkin he'd wedged in his shirt and followed Zeke into the bar. Zeke took a table for two next to a large aquarium and ordered fresh drinks.

"Despite what you read in the tabloids," Zeke said, "I don't usually promote exchanging favors when it has to do with my movies."

Junior cleared his throat. "Don't go the money route. Brinkman's already told me about your offer to him. He reported it like a good soldier."

"I'm not talking money, chief."

"What else is there?"

"Because I want this film to be shot here so badly, I'm prepared to offer you something better than money?"

"What's better?"

"Sex."

"Oh...ah...I don't know about that, Clayton."

Zeke took a long tug on his drink. "When's the last time you and Eileen...you know?"

The chief squirmed slightly in his chair and cleared his throat. "It's not as bad as you might think, Clayton. She's had a long bout with depression and has let herself go a little, but —"

"But you haven't touched her since Clinton-Gore. Right?"

"Doesn't mean I go without," Junior shot back.

Zeke could tell by the chief's uneasy eyes and the sweat on his lip that he was on the defensive. "Tell you what, Chief. I've got a deal for you."

"I don't do deals, Clayton."

"Hear me out," Zeke said. "I think you'll like what I'm offering." Zeke tapped out a drum roll on the table with both his index fingers. "In exchange for allowing me to shoot my movie in your town, I'll give you Lonnie."

Junior's eyebrows sprung to attention. "You mean –"

"I mean 24/7, chief. She'd be at your beck and call. Here or in L.A., whichever suits you best: sweet and yet discreet. Your wife will never know."

Chief McWorter Jr. exhaled deeply, blowing air through his lips. "Let me get back to –"

"Sorry, Chief. It's a one time only offer."

The chief scratched at his temple. "I see how you got the reputation as a great dealmaker, Clayton."

"Then it's a deal."

"How long do I have access to Lonnie?"

"Until my film is released. That could take two years."

"Deal," Junior said, extending a hand that was wet from perspiration.

They agreed to discuss the particulars at a later time, finished their drinks and rejoined the ladies for dinner. The chief was downright affable upon his return.

When they finally parted company the chief thanked Zeke for his generosity and winked, saying, "I'll be in touch."

"I'm sure you will," Zeke said with a big smile.

Junior looked back at Zeke who was still working out the tip at the table. "Just curious," he said, "anyone ever ask you where you were that night in June of '62?"

Zeke's eyebrows squeezed at one another as he glanced at Lonnie. "Can't say they ever did, Chief."

CHAPTER 21

C ecil was snoring so bad Vernon had to ratchet up the sound on the TV to hear anything. At the moment, a dark haired woman anchor with lips the size of air mattresses was previewing the top stories for the eleven-o'clock news. A graphic identified her as Rita Arenas.

"…Plus, we'll hear from a jailed Carpenteria woman who meant business when she said no to her neighbor's sexual advances and plugged him a dozen times with a handgun. And, speaking of business, Lance Vance will report live from the Sea Breeze motel on upper State Street, where a handful of members of the infamous San Marcos High School class of '62 are holding their first-ever reunion, selling out the motel for the night, but possibly setting up the owner for a consumer backlash that could ruin his business. That plus the 5-day forecast for the Central Coast and Matt Bianchi on sports with the wacky story about a women's softball MVP who is switching so she can swing like a man. The complete stories…"

As Rita's image faded into a commercial, Vernon shot up in bed, clicked off the set with the remote and hollered for Cecil to wake up.

Nothing.

"Wake up you lazy bastard, "Vernon repeated. "You make one stinking haul a day and you're so tired you go into a coma. I swear I'm going to find me a younger partner, one who doesn't need to have Amtrak run over his chest to wake him up."

"Yes. Oh, yes!" Cecil shouted as he tossed his covers off him to the other side of the bed."

"Sleeping Beauty has awakened," Vernon said.

Cecil wiped his swollen eyes and then stretched his arms and back. "Damn, just when a dark skinned super model was about to go down on me. Why does that always happen to me, Vernon? It's depressing."

"You're disgusting, Cecil. You snore like you're trying to suck worms up your nose. God, it's distracting. No wonder you can't get a woman besides Francis McCarthy."

"Shut up with the Francis McCarthy talk," Cecil said.

Vernon was satisfied that he'd finally captured his partner's attention. "Christ, I couldn't sleep at all so I got up and watched the news. And, guess what I learned?"

"Tell me so I can go back to sleep."

"You're not going back to sleep after what I learned."

"You're talking crazy, Vernon. I'm going back to sleep as soon as you stop talking to me."

"You have to listen to me, Cecil."

"You've got thirty seconds. Then I'm calling the manager and demanding he give me another room. Screw our operating budget. Some expenses aren't worth sparing."

"That's just it, Cecil. There are no rooms available. I heard it on the news."

"Then I'll sleep in the van."

"Forget the sleeping, already. We've got work to do."

"Explain."

"All the rooms are taken by people attending that reunion in the activity center."

"So?"

"Jeez Louise! I gotta think for the both us. All the time it's like this."

"Stop with the whining, Vernon. It makes you so Jewish."

"Don't you get it, Cecil. If everyone who's staying here tonight is attending the reunion then his or her room is likely to be empty until at least midnight. We've got *carte blanche*, my friend. We can steal enough stuff – coats, jewelry, laptops, iPads to cover our Vegas expenses. We could do it in an hour."

Cecil scratched at the base of his ear. "This is good thinking, Vernon."

"Of course it is."

"But, if I hadn't been snoring…"

"There you go, trying to take the credit for everything, Cecil."

"Credit where credit is due is what makes this country strong."

"Can you just shut up, Cecil, and find your tools. We haven't got all night."

CHAPTER 22

She didn't know if she would ever be able to adequately express her gratitude for her family's help in setting her up with her own restaurant, but Cha Cha Miranda was determined to show it with a grand fiesta: a celebration of the official opening of Casa de Cha Cha. Even with part-time help from her mother, it had taken her over a month to plan. She'd booked the best Mariachi band on the Central Coast plus a touring dance troupe from Mexico City. The best Mexican artist in Santa Barbara, Alfredo Morales, committed to exhibit a small collection of his work. The public would have to wait a night; the fiesta was for family and friends only – all two hundred of them.

Ignacio and Maria Consuela Miranda, both still vibrant although now in their mid-eighties, had been deeply disappointed and embarrassed that they weren't able to send Cha Cha to a four-year university.

"College of Hard Knocks is all we can afford," Ignacio had said apologetically. "I'll make it up to you somehow, baby," he promised her. Ignacio had come to accept that a Mexican in the States, whose workers – most of them family members – were undocumented, would always be a gardener rather than a landscaper. But to his credit, he came up with an alternative plan. Ignacio worked out an arrangement with his cousin Amelia in Guadalarja. He would send his daughter to work in Amelia's restaurant in exchange for room and board. Both Ignacio and Maria Consuela believed that if Cha Cha applied herself, she could learn everything there was to know about running a restaurant and perhaps, one day set up her own in Santa Barbara. Cha Cha was excited about the opportunity.

Learn she did: how to make real Mexican *tacos, tamales, enchiladas, carnitas, quesadillas, mole, Hominy stew, flan, and arroz con leche.*

Equally important, Cha Cha learned how to buy liquor and run the restaurant's bar. In two years, she doubled the bar's revenues.

After working for Amelia for almost ten years – Tortilla Tech she called it – Cha Cha believed she was ready to run a place of her own. She returned to Santa Barbara and with the help of her parents and extended family, was able to raise enough money to pay the first three months rent on a place near East Beach that had most recently been a hamburger joint. Ironically, the guy who'd operated Hamburger Haven was an acquaintance. Charles Viniterri had been the head of the senior social activities committee at San Marcos during the 1961-62 school year. Cha Cha had served on a similar committee at Santa Barbara High that year. The two bodies worked together one time to hold a dance between the two schools. According to the leasing agent, Viniterri was forced out of business because of a string of County Health Services violations that included the discovery of a King snake in the women's toilet.

When she was told about Viniterri's bad luck, Cha Cha almost decided against setting up her restaurant there. She weighed her decision for weeks until another party expressed an interest in snapping up the place. She had trouble coming to terms with yet another member of the San Marcos class of '62 having a run of bad luck. Even during the years she was in Mexico, she'd managed to get word from family and former classmates about how bad things in general were going for kids from that class.

Cadillac margaritas were on the house at Cha Cha's fiesta. It was a great way —expensive as it was – for her to introduce people to her many house specialties. No one took advantage of the offer more than the hostess. Cha Cha poured down the margaritas like her supply of tequila would spoil over night. When she wasn't drinking and glad-handing with her guests, she was dancing – mostly with her dad and Punky Grayson, her best friend since the second grade. Cha Cha and Punky, whose real name was Elizabeth, had practiced so many times over the years they could do the Mexican Hat Dance together with their eyes closed.

Long after the fiesta ended Punky stayed to help Cha Cha clean up. Casa de Cha Cha was to open to the general public in less than twelve hours. After five hours of intense partying the place was trashed.

"I wouldn't have guessed two hundred people could make such a mess," Cha Cha said to her friend.

"If they drank half as much as you, I could understand," Punky said, smiling as she wiped chimichanga crumbs from a beer stained tabletop.

"I drank from happiness," Punky. "You, of all people, know I don't usually drink so much. There is just so much for me to be thankful for. It overwhelmed me."

113

"Then, how come every time I turned around you had tears in your eyes."

"Because I was drinking from sorrow too."

Cha Cha found an abandoned margarita on the floor next to one of the tables and took a big swallow from the half-empty glass.

"Ooh! How can you do that?" Punky said.

"I do crazy things when I'm depressed."

"Two seconds ago you were telling me how happy you were tonight."

"I'm capable of many things, Punky."

"Cha Cha. I've known you long enough, there's something tugging at you."

Cha Cha inspected what was left of her adopted margarita. "It's this place, Punky."

"This is a great place. You will enjoy nothing but success. Your menu is great, the location is great, being next to the Sterns Wharf and all. And, you've got the energy of five people."

"I'm just sad for the guy who was here before me."

"Good God. Why? He made his own bed with sloppy management."

Cha Cha began to cry.

Punky waited for her to stop. "Something's definitely got hold of you, Cha Cha. You want to talk about it? That's what best friends are for."

"No...no thanks," Cha Cha said, giving a backhand wave to her friend. "It's just that...people like Charles Viniterri have been cursed because of me."

"You're not making sense," Cha Cha.

Cha Cha stopped crying and dabbed at her wet eyes with a tissue. "If I hadn't kept it a secret, maybe none of this would have happened."

"Kept what a secret?"

Cha Cha's eyes dropped. "If I told you it wouldn't be a secret anymore, would it?"

"Now, you're acting strange. And I don't think it's the margaritas. This is like watching a bad movie, Cha Cha."

"Trust me, Punky, it was a bad movie."

CHAPTER 23

With Mustafa Muhammad serving as a mediator – he was afraid of losing his "sweet thing" to an assault charge – Dee Dee and Lance Vance worked out a compromise. Lance could do his interviews and live hit, but not from inside the activity center. He agreed to set up his camera in the parking lot and shoot back at the entrance to the building. The other concession Dee Dee made was strictly cosmetic – she agreed to allow Lance to use the activity center men's room to put on his makeup before going on camera.

When Dee Dee returned to the party she was shocked to see Vaughn Berglund's wheelchair being parked opposite Whitney Crawford's chair in the middle of the circle of classmates. She turned to Mustafa with a chin that had dropped. "What do I do?"

Mustafa's brow flexed. "Ask them if they're comfortable with the situation. If they are then let's revisit our little love nest on the second floor."

"I just want to punch the guy," Dee Dee said.

To her own surprise, Dee Dee followed Mustafa's suggestion, asking for quiet from her classmates as she approached Whitney and Vaughn Berglund.

"How many people are okay with Whitney cross examining Vaughn?" she said. "Raise your hands."

Not one hand was held back.

Reno approached the three of them. "He's already grilled me. The wheels are already in motion, Dee Dee. It's harmless, actually."

"What was your outcome?" Dee Dee said to Reno.

"Did Not Do It!" Reno said, stretching out each word.

Dee Dee shook her head then rolled her eyes. "If this is okay with everybody, then who am I to interfere?" She turned and started to walk away. "But I won't be a party to it. Especially when you're asking questions of someone who doesn't know what planet he's on. It's degrading."

"Some folks say I'm kinda out there," Reno interrupted. "And I went through it."

Dee Dee hiked her shoulders. "If you need me," she said, "the manager knows how to reach me."

"You and Mustafa are what the folks in my neck of the woods call 'swirlers'," Reno said, eyeing both.

"Swingers," Edgar Peoples shouted.

"Damn it, Edgar," Reno said with a smile. "Go sit down and with your fingers and toes count the number of times you've interrupted me tonight."

Edgar presented Reno with an "I'm not worthy" gesture from his seat.

"Swirlers," Reno continued, "are a little bit vanila, a little bit chocolate, which means that when they make love, it's twice as sweet."

Dee Dee waited for the laughter to quiet then offered a sly smile while taking Mustafa by the hand and heading for the side exit.

She never made it out of the building, however. Greeting her at the door, his feet planted shoulder width apart and his necked bowed in a General Patton-like stance, was Police Chief Franklin McWorter, Jr. and a posse of three.

"Well, a pleasant how-do-you-do, Chief McWorter, Jr.," Dee Dee said. "To what do we owe the pleasure of your company?"

"You're going to owe your parole officer an explanation if you continue to be a smart mouth, lady."

"You'll excuse me for not realizing that a friendly greeting is a felony."

The chief turned to one of his posse and said loud enough for anyone in the activity center to hear, "Have Sergeant Strickland bring in the dog."

At the mention of a dog, Lance Vance, his cameraman in tow, burst into the room with videotape rolling. Lance positioned himself in front of the camera so that any police activity would be in the picture behind him. He took a small hairbrush out of his pocket, swiped at his blonde locks a couple of times and said, "Police Chief Franklin McWorter, Jr. himself directed the raid shortly after nine o'clock – "

"Get the fuck out of here," Dee Dee screamed at Lance. She glanced at Mustafa as if to read his intentions and then advanced on the reporter herself. "You fucking lying sack of shit."

Without turning away from the camera, Lance motioned for Dee Dee to stop screaming. "Could you hear the fuck part in your headset?" he asked his cameraman. When he got a nod in the affirmative, Lance started over. "Shortly after nine o'clock Police Chief Franklin McWorter, Jr..."

The chief's command and the appearance of the TV camera created a giant buzz among the attendees and set Wayne Preston into a code three retreat. His face as gray as the metal chair from which he bolted, Wayne hurdled a TV tray full of abandoned drinks, sidestepped around the bar, bumped into Anthony Castello, who'd come to count the house again, then sprinted, as best he could for someone battling an acute arthritis condition, toward the entrance. But just before he got there, a fast charging German Shepard clamped onto his pants pocket and dragged him to the floor like he was constructed of Papier Mache.

"I've got stuff, okay?" Wayne yelled. "I confess. Guilty. Guilty." The German Shepard now had his teeth wrapped around Wayne's collar and was administering an effective chokehold. "Get this beast off me, okay? Please. I said I've got stuff."

A smiling Chief McWorter, Jr. finally ordered his sergeant to take control of the dog, then approached Wayne. "What am I going to find in your possession?" the chief said.

"Grass," Wayne said meekly.

"How much you got on you?"

"Around an ounce."

The chief's smile broadened. "Take him and book him," he said to a posse member as he picked Wayne off the floor by his jacket lapels. "Sergeant Strickland, take the dog and mingle with the guests." He then turned and addressed the group. "Anybody else got anything on 'em?" He waited for a response. There was none. "Believe me, you don't want the dog to find it."

Reno raised a hand but spoke before being acknowledged. "I'm packin' a condom. Is that legal in this cow town?"

Chief McWorte,r Jr., the smirk on his face gone, walked over to Reno and gave him a thorough once over with his piercing eyes. "It's a societal phenomena, anytime you get more than a half-dozen people together you get at least one smart ass," the chief said to the group. He moved his face up in Reno's grill. "You're that smart ass, pal. Just looking at that beer gut of yours, I can't imagine you'd ever get any use out of a condom unless you were planning a water balloon fight."

Reno dropped to his knees and moaned like someone who been kicked in the balls. "You've ruined my prospects, officer."

The chief returned to where Wayne Preston was being cuffed and again addressed the group. He wore a broad smile. "I will ruin the night for each and every one of you if I get as much as one complaint about noise coming from this building. You class of '62 people are..." He thought it, but he avoided using the word losers. It's actually a good thing that you're all in the same room together. That way you can only harm each other."

No sooner had the chief made his exit than Reno stood up and said, "Don't be intimidated by that cop. He's had an entire career to figure out who's responsible for the *skin flick* and all they have to show for it is a giant case of the 'red ass'."

Applause filled the room.

"Shall we continue?" Whitney Crawford said to the group.

"Do whatever you want," Dee Dee Wellborn said, flipping off Lance Vance as she and Mustafa exited.

Moments later the unmistakable high-pitched voice of Wayne Preston could be heard from outside the activity center. "Hear me brothers and sisters! Hear me! My vote is for Vaughn Berglund."

The sound of a police siren drowned out an exchange of obscenities.

CHAPTER 24

"I shall not seek, and I will not accept, the nomination of my party for another term as your president." President Lyndon Johnson's words in March of 1968 echoed in Private Edgar Peoples' head for days. From Edgar's perspective, it signaled the country was in such deep shit in Vietnam that LBJ didn't think he had a shovel big enough. It wasn't good news for Private Peoples or anyone in Company C, first battalion, 184th infantry division California National Guard, headquartered in Santa Barbara. They had long been rumored to be at the top of the list of reserve units destined for Vietnam duty.

Everyone in Private Peoples' unit arrived early for the first Saturday formation in April of 1968. That had never happened before. Anywhere from a half dozen to a dozen members of Company C were habitually late arrivals. As the company's four platoon's readied for roll call this day, Private Peoples' could tell by the strained look on so many of his buddy's faces that anxiety was running high. It was as if every single one of his fellow weekend warriors had heard the rumors on the news or read about them in the paper.

"Fuck," Private Warren Harris whispered, "this unit is heading over the pond by summer as sure as I'm standing here, and now my girlfriend tells me she's pregnant." He shook his head so that his steel pot swiveled. "Why can't I catch a fucking break?"

Aware that Company C's officers were running behind schedule for roll call, Private Peoples answered Harris in a normal voice. "You can't do anything about the war, so stop whining." Edgar then leaned close to Private Harris' ear and whispered. "But you sure as shit ought to test for paternity. Don't be stupid. There are ladies out their fooling guys all the time."

Private Harris ignored the remark, choosing instead to inspect the chamber of his M-16. He blew into it and debris flew out. "Still clean enough to kill Charlie, I'm guessing."

"Christ, I hope I never have to go on patrol with you, Harris, not with your maintenance standards. I might as well paint a target on my chest."

"And patrolling is what we'll be doing," Private Harris whispered back. "Don't forget, this company is twenty percent class of '62. We're sure to get fucked. Tell me, Peoples, you think it's a coincidence that every swingin' dick from San Marcos '62 has been funneled into this unit instead of that lame ass transportation outfit in Carpenteria?"

"Do you know that to be a fact, Harris?"

"My dad researched it. He's still trying to get me out on account someone is manipulating the assignment process."

"You really think, Harris?"

"Damn straight."

"You should have your old man fight it, too. Being colored and all, you might have an even better chance of getting transferred out of here. Reverse discrimination."

"Being colored and all, my old man skipped when I was three."

The day before Edgar's unit was due to report to Fort Ord for four weeks of intensive training before shipping out to Vietnam, Janet Nyborg received a letter from him. Grandma Ruth was frying chicken on her new electric burners when Janet burst into the kitchen holding the opened envelope high to the heavens. "Grandma," she said between rushes of tears. "There is a God."

"What is it, darlin'?"

"It's college for Lance," Janet said, between breaths. She pulled a cashier's check for seventy thousand dollars out of the envelope.

"I do declare, Janet, this is wonderful. But it does require some explaining don't you think?" Ruth wiped her hands on her apron and then surprised Janet with a hug. "God, don't let your Grandpa Joe know about this or he'll be wanting some of it for past expenses. Do you know what I'm saying?"

Janet nodded.

"I guess you'll tell me who the money is from in due time."

"I can't do that, Grandma Ruth."

Ruth turned and walked back to her simmering chicken. Each time she pushed a piece with her fork, grease spit into the air. After several minutes of silence Ruth said, "It's legal and all, isn't it, Janet?"

Figuring she'd shared enough about her good fortune with her grandmother Janet confirmed that it was a gift and then moved in the direction of the bathroom where she knew she could close the door and escape any more scrutiny.

Just as Janet was about to close the bathroom door, Grandma Ruth said, "Aren't you going to tell me who it's from, darlin'? It's not every day someone in this neck of the woods gets that kind of money."

"Maybe one day I'll be able to tell you, Grandma. But, not now."

"But, child – "

Janet turned and took several steps back toward Ruth. "It's about Lance. That's all you need to know. It's all anyone needs to know."

"Have it your way, dear."

Janet retreated to the bathroom where she closed the door and once more examined the contents of the letter that had accompanied the check.

Dear Janet,

My unit's headed over the pond. I figured I needed to take care of business before I leave on Saturday. Enclosed you'll find a check that should cover much of our son's college. Just reminding you to keep a lid on things. One slip of the tongue and we all go down. I hope you will eventually see fit to allow young Lance into my life. I hope he grows up to be a great athlete like I never was. I do know that with our mix, he's going to be a great looking kid. Good Luck to both you and Lance,

Private Edgar

Janet methodically crumpled Edgar's letter into something the size of a baseball and deposited it in the toilet. She cried out loud as she pulled the flush handle.

CHAPTER 25

Edgar was sitting on the hood of his midnight blue 2007 Jeep Grand Cherokee that he'd strategically parked in the Sea Breeze lot when he noticed a couple of old guys acting suspicious on the second floor balcony. His muscles tensed at the discovery. He dragged hard on his cigarette as he watched their movements. Ever since Vietnam, Edgar had been suspicious of everything and everyone. He'd logged lots of hours on shrinks' couches as a result. He readily admits that his suspicious nature is why he's never married. He chased off the only steady he ever had – a professional Tango dancer named Evita – because she mistakenly called him Edward one night when they were making love. Even on the job he's suspicious – he administers eye tests for the DMW; has for twenty years. He tells anyone who'll listen, "It's a dead-end job that's lasted twenty years. He claims many of his co-workers pocket registration fees; not to mention take more breaks than they're allowed. "It explains how the DMV is the black hole of the bureaucratic process," he's said repeatedly over the years.

While tracking the two old guy's Edgar noticed that one of them, the shorter of the two, kept looking over his shoulder as the two reached the door to the last room on the floor. He thought it odd that they weren't carrying luggage, only a small case. He figured it for either a tool kit or a medicine bag. Doctors don't make house calls in pairs, he reasoned, ruling out the latter. Just as Edgar's curiosity was piquing, Darlene Kauffman wandered out of the activity center and walked in his direction. It changed his whole focus.

Darlene had been the social committee chairman their senior year. She was in charge of all senior activities. It was a big responsibility. At 5'11" Darlene was taller than most girls; that made her a natural for the volleyball team. She had dark skin, large breasts and a seductive smile that was beyond her appeal. She'd been a steady of the tight end on the football team for most of her senior year but broke up him a month before graduation.

Darlene had surprised Edgar by coming onto him during a senior class event near the end of the '62 school year. It was a car wash fund-raiser.

"I really believe Martin Luther King has a vision," she said out of the blue while they were wiping down the same hubcap.

"What makes you say that at this particular time, Darlene?"

"Because I want you to know I'm not a racist."

"I never said you were."

Darlene then placed her face so close to Edgar's he could smell the Sin Sin's on her breath. "It's just my way of telling you I'd like to experience a black dick before I graduate."

Edgar gagged on his saliva, which Darlene took for a yes. That night she surprised him by picking him up at home in her '56 Chevy and taking him to park at Goleta Beach where she got the experience she was looking for.

As he assessed her decades later, Edgar gave Darlene a passing grade. Her hair was salt and pepper and her hips were a little big, but she still had the same sultry smile, and tits that appeared not to have fallen like so many of the other women he'd observed tonight.

"Contemplating life as you know it?" Darlene greeted him.

"Just watching to see what those two old farts on the balcony are up to," Edgar said, pointing his burning cigarette in their direction.

"I'd say they're about to rip off someone's room," Darlene said.

"My thoughts exactly."

"I spent ten years with the Sheriff's department, until I got caught snorting evidence. I can spot a burglary attempt a mile away."

"Shouldn't we do something about it?"

"Nah. I didn't come out here to catch a thief."

"What did you come for?"

"I wanted to see you. You've been ignoring me all night. It's been a long time, Edgar."

"It has."

For the first time since she'd approached him, Edgar noticed Darlene's wedding band. "Who's the lucky guy?" he said, allowing his eyes to track to her hand.

"A department veteran. Retired."

"How come he's not here tonight?"

"He takes advantages of opportunities like this to spend with his forty-year old girlfriend."

"Ooh," Edgar said, lighting another cigarette.

"So what do you think, Edgar? Have I still got it?" Darlene pulled her black shawl off her shoulders, revealing even more cleavage.

"Most definitely," Edgar said, suddenly worried where Darlene was going with the conversation. "Listen, I've got to run back inside," Edgar said, tossing his unfinished cigarette to the ground. "It's been fun catching up with you –"

"But, I'm making you nervous, being married and all." Darlene smiled.

"You could say that."

"From what I've observed you've been stressed all night, Edgar. I thought you were going to have a seizure when you found out your name was on that ballot."

"It's that Whitney guy. He wanted a piece of me because I'm black."

"I can remember a time when a young senior classmate of yours wanted a piece of you too," Darlene said with a whisper. "And, if memory serves me, she got it."

Edgar shuffled his feet slightly as he considered a response. "That was then, this is now," he said, and walked off toward the activity center without a good-bye. By the time he reached the entrance the two old guys were a distant memory.

CHAPTER 26

Cecil figured luck was on their side when the first room he and Vernon tried, number 204, a suite, was unlocked. "I think the stars are aligned just right for us, Vernon."

"Fuck the stars, Cecil. Someone's been in this bed. But there aren't any personal effects, no clothes, no luggage, nothing. Christ!" Vernon interrupted himself with a discovery. "There's a fucking condom next to the pillow that's still got some guy's juice on it."

"Who pays for a room just to fuck?" Cecil said.

"Usually people having affairs. They don't even bring a toothbrush."

"You ever have and affair, Vernon?"

"What the fuck, Cecil, this is no time for a morality test."

"I'll bet you never did."

"Not that I couldn't have."

"I knew it. I could tell you were afraid of Alma; rest her soul. She'd have beaten you to within an inch of your life if she'd caught you dippin' your ink in some other well."

Vernon took a quick look around the rest of the suite and reported finding nothing to steal.

"Then let's at least take the TV, Vernon. It's a Sony. Probably get two hundred for it."

"Fuck the TV. How are we going to haul it out of here without being noticed. It's one thing to be carrying luggage, but a fuckin' TV? We might as well tie cow bells to our – "

"Shit!" Cecil said. "You hear that?"

"Yeah. Sounds like two people."

"You think they're coming in here, Vernon?"

"They're getttin' closer, dammit.

On Vernon's cue the two scrambled for the bedroom closet as best two guys their ages could hurry. No sooner had they untangled themselves in their tiny hiding place than they heard the same voices now coming from the bedroom, no more than ten feet away – a man's and a woman's. But then the voices fell silent. All either Vernon or Cecil could hear was the feint sounds of what they both assumed were clothes being removed.

"Let me start on top this time," they heard the woman say.

"We goin' round the world this time, sweet thing?" the man said.

"And back," the woman said.

The talking stopped within seconds. All Vernon and Cecil could hear now was the bed squeaking. "I hope the guy's got a quick release," Cecil whispered. "Cause I can't stay in this position long without my knees exploding."

132

"You don't have much choice unless you want to be arrested for breaking and entering."

"We didn't break into anything. It was open."

"Tell that to the judge. Now shut up before they hear us."

"I can't believe how big you feel," Vernon and Cecil heard the woman say. She was breathing heavy.

"You make me that way, baby," the man said. "Ride the rail, baby. Ride the rail."

"Oh, God! You fill all of me. Ooh! Aah! I'm gonna – "

"Wait for me, baby. I'm close. Aah!"

Cecil squinted to look at Vernon in the dark. "I'm gonna' cum before either of them."

"I'll bet that wand of yours doesn't even work anymore. They say after seventy it can go kaput on you without warning. Now, shut up."

The sound of the headboard banging against the wall made it impossible for Vernon and Cecil to hear one another any longer.

"My God. Where have you been all my life?" the woman said.

"Just growin' large for the right time, baby."

"Aah."

"Ooh!"

"Aah! Ooh!"

"Yes!"

"Fuck me harder."

"It's happening, baby."

"Me too!"

"Uuhhhhhhhh!"

"Uuhhhhhhhh!"

There was silence outside the closet – except for heavy breathing

The next sound came from inside the closet. "Uuhhhhhhh!"

"Fuck, Cecil! You idiot!"

"I warned you, Vernon."

The woman spoke louder than at any time. "Did you hear that?"

"What?" the man said, still breathing heavily.

"Someone's in this bedroom," she said, her voice rising even more.

Vernon whispered to Cecil who was inspecting his wet crotch. "We're fucked because of you."

The man said, "It's coming from the closet."

Vernon and Cecil could hear someone get off the bed.

"Why's it always the man who has to stick his neck out and risk getting shot?" the man said.

Just then, there was a heavy knock on the door to the suite.

"Who's there?" the woman said.

"It's Anthony. I'm sorry to bother you but I have a message for you."

"In the bedroom," the woman shouted. "Quick!"

The closet door slid open maybe an inch; just enough for Vernon and Cecil to make out a black man with eye whites as big as volleyballs.

"Don't see anyone in here," the man said. Fortunately, Vernon and Cecil were hunkered down behind the sliding door at the other end of the closet. As soon as they saw the image of the new arrival pass before them, they opened their end of the closet and tried desperately to unravel their cramped bodies from the tiny space they'd occupied.

"My back," Cecil moaned.

"My leg," Vernon whimpered.

"My balls," Cecil cried.

"That's your fault, asshole," Vernon complained.

The man who answered to Anthony said, "The musicians want to play or they want to go home,"

"Fuck them," Dee Dee said. "Oh! There's the bastard," she said, seeing Cecil dart out the bedroom door.

"What bastard?" Anthony said, unable to turn around fast enough to observe anyone.

"No, there are two of them," the woman shouted as Vernon made his exit. "Call the cops! Thieves! Stop them, Mustafa!"

"Shit!" Mustafa said, hopping back in bed.

"Go after them!" Dee Dee screamed at Mustafa. "Christ, you know Tae Kwon Do."

"Oh, no, baby. I never expose my bare piece to the elements or place it in harms way. Not for nothing. It's a valuable possession, in case you haven't noticed. Some people protect their jewels. I look after my piece."

"Jesus Christ!" Dee Dee said grabbing at her hair with both hands. "Why, just once God, can't I ever have it all?"

Mustafa rolled to his side of the bed. 'Besides, I don't know Tae Kwan Do, I just know the business of selling it."

Dee Dee sighed and let her body flop against the headboard. "Jesus, this man who has a dick big enough for the Smithsonian, has no balls. Go figure."

CHAPTER 27

Linda Dalby Yarnell had never driven Laurel Canyon's winding two-lane road. Because of all the turns, the traffic was slow. She was seldom able to push her new '69 Corvette in excess of 45 mph, which frustrated her. The time it took made her anxious as well. She worried she'd be late for her interview at Noonan-Bryce Studios. The Natalie Woods, Faye Dunaways and Ali McGraws had licenses to be late, but not someone with one lonesome screen credit too many years ago.

Linda had been energized by her decision to try and rekindle her acting career, even if her husband of two months wasn't happy about it. Howard Yarnell wanted to raise a family. Linda, who was only twenty-six, figured she still had time to make babies. Through an awakening she attributed to practicing TM – she still remembers her mantra today – Linda was able to rationalize her persistent desire for a movie career. Sitting on the sidelines and unhappily playing the socially active housewife during her failed first marriage – until Bernie the record exec bought the big house – had made her rethink her future. She only wished she'd been honest and disclosed her feelings to Howard when she agreed to marry him.

"Mr. Noonan will see you now, Ms. Dalby," the secretary with white French Poodle designs on her pink skirt said while looking over what Linda figured to be a take out lunch menu. "That way," she said, pointing to the door to her right without ever looking up.

Linda took a deep breath and stepped that way. She'd rehearsed the interview process a thousand times in her mind. Poise was the key. She was convinced that every great actress had that attribute. Her physical appearance would speak for itself. Linda had lost ten pounds for this very moment and she believed she'd never looked better. Her hip size was no longer a problem. She was tan, tantalizing in a red Saint Laurent and, of course, talented.

Felton Noonan was a tall, distinguished looking man of 60 – maybe a few years more, Linda guessed. He had a moustache and wore his slightly graying hair down to his collar. His smile was warm, his greeting friendly.

"Thank you for freeing up time on short notice to meet with me," Linda said, taking a chair opposite his massive cherry wood executive desk.

"I have time for any client of Sally Walker's."

"It's comforting to know my agent has a nice reputation. I know that's not always the case in this town."

"No truer words have been spoken."

Felton lit a Viceroy and got up out of his chair. He turned his back to Linda to look out the window of his seventh floor suite. Linda did not like the sudden change in his dynamics.

"I've seen tape of your *Fugitive* episode. I've watched your most recent screen test. No question you have the talent for this business."

Linda fidgeted with the handle on her purse. "Why do I sense there is a but coming?"

"Your instincts are good, Ms. Dalby."

"Give it to me straight, Mr. Noonan."

He moved away from the window and sat on the corner of his desk. He looked down at her. Linda recognized it as a power position.

"This is a town of lists as I'm sure you know if you've studied its history," he said. "Goes clear back to Hollywood's blacklist days. There are good lists and bad lists. It's not just for actors and actresses. There are lists for directors, cinema photographers, casting agents, etc. Follow me?"

Linda nodded. Her eyes no longer sparkled; her lower lip was turned down.

"Well, your name has preceded your visit."

"I'm on the bad list, I take it."

Felton nodded his head in the affirmative. He took a deep breath and continued. "There are never any reasons cited for someone being on a list; good one or bad. It's just the way it is. The practice is accepted. Only the identity of the person who submitted a name to a list is made known."

"Who on earth even knows me in this – "

"It wouldn't be ethical of me to disclose –"

"My God. Could it be Zeke Clayton? We went to high school together for a year." Linda put her hand to her mouth, which was agape.

Felton eyebrows spiked. "It could be. That's all I'm going to say."

Linda sat silently for a moment, staring out the window at nothing. Finally, she stood up and looked deep into Felton's eyes. "Tell me yes or no, please. My movie career is over before it's had a chance to begin because Zeke Clayton has my name on his bad list? Is that it? I need to hear the words."

"At the top."

Linda was at once angered by the words and strangely relieved as well. She'd been emotionally scarred at seeing her nude body appear in Zeke Clayton's shower film. Deep down she'd wondered if she could perform nude for Hollywood. She finally responded to Felton Noonan. "He's got that kind of clout?"

"Ever since he won Best Picture for *After Midnight*. He's the boy genius, you know."

"I guess a leopard never changes his spots."

"Not in this industry, Ms. Dalby."

CHAPTER 28

Linda Dalby returned from the bar with a bottle of mineral water in each hand. After planting a wet kiss on his lips, she gave one to Scott and set the other next to her chair. She felt uncomfortable sharing Scott with her classmates. Their conversations, in the brief time they'd known each other had always been so intimate. Linda had been intrigued by the fact that in just a couple of weeks Scott had come to know more about her than either of her husbands.

"Knock yourself out," she said as she watched Scott chug his water.

"It's what recovering addicts do," he said through wet lips.

"I'd like to do you," Linda said purring in his ear.

"My shrink warns me that you're all about getting even with my dad."

"Your shrink has never seen me in bed."

"A point well taken." Scott took another tug on his water.

Linda was mildly disturbed by Whitney Crawford's turning the party into *The People's Court*. She wanted time with Scott not *Matlock*. But Linda, along with the rest of her classmates, seemed more willing to accept Whitney's agenda, with Dee Dee's presence reduced to near non-existent.

Linda's heart went out to Vaughn Berglund as he vegetated in his wheelchair opposite Whitney in the inner circle. He was still slumped forward, his empty eyes fixed on the floor. "I'll be glad when this is over," she said to Scott.

"Me too," he said.

Linda watched with growing curiosity as Whitney set the ground rules for his cross-examination of Vaughn.

"There are certain facts that I must establish and then I am going to try and stir a response from Berglund," Whitney said.

A collective gasp could be heard from all over the room.

"We know the following to be fact." Whitney held up a small whiteboard with bullet points running top to bottom. *Vaughn Berglund Talking Points* the whiteboard read. Whitney went through the list point by point:

"Student head of the audio-visual department. Was a known fuck-off. Set school record with 82 demerits by the end of his junior year. Had just broken up with Wendy Overton and skipped senior party. Lived only half a mile from KEYT's studio. Had parents who could afford to have something kept quiet."

A voice from behind Whitney punctuated his reading of the list. "Let's juice him now and get to partying." Linda didn't recognize the voice, but it was a guy. The suggestion made her cringe.

Linda, like the majority of her classmates, had observed Whitney studying Vaughn's eyes, as he'd read through his list. She figured him to be like a mad scientist toiling in his lab. But there was no response from Vaughn. After pausing to sip water, Whitney trumpeted the next phase of his presentation by uncovering some items he'd placed on a small coffee table next to him.

"Berglund if you recognize any of these items and it triggers a response, just blink your eyes."

Scott turned to Linda and whispered, "How sick is this?"

"Extremely," she said, shaking her head.

Whitney picked up an open film canister and placed it opposite Vaughn's chest. "Berglund," he said, "do you recognize this film as the one you placed in KEYT's master control film chain?"

No response.

Whitney picked up a badly wrinkled ticket stub. "Do you recognize this as your ticket stub to *The Princess Blows Through Town*, a porno movie which you attended with Elmer LaCoss on June 12, 1962 at the Roxie Theatre on Milpas?"

Nothing from Vaughn.

Whitney turned his attention to his classmates. "This is not designed to be cruel and unusual punishment," he said, "although some of you will consider it such. Last month's edition of *Psychiatry Today* contains a story about 'article recognition' that is amazing. Researchers at UC Med Center actually tested patients who'd suffered varying degrees of brain damage and found that seventy-five percent of them did demonstrate a measurable response to certain relevant items like photos, mementos and keepsakes."

What Linda Dalby heard next out of the mouth of Reno Parris jolted her.

"How about we get Wendy Overton up and see if Vaughn recognizes her bare titties? That would be the litany test."

"Litmus," Whitney said, shaking his head.

Linda hadn't realized Wendy was sitting right behind her until she heard her shriek. She would never have recognized her. The years had been unkind to a woman who, so many years ago personified "cute" – bobbed nose, bangs, electric smile.

"This is insane," Wendy said, her words choked by emotion. Impulsively, she jumped up from her chair and ran toward the inner circle where Whitney and Vaughn faced one another. "How's this?" she said, pulling her purple silk blouse over her head and unsnapping her bra. "Will this really help?" she said, addressing the group rather than any one person. Without waiting for a response, Wendy crouched in front of Vaughn's wheelchair and delicately raised his chin with her hand. "Recognize these babies, Vaughn?" she said. "Of course you don't." Wendy choked on her words. "I wouldn't expect you to after a butchered boob job here." Wendy squeezed her left breast. "And a mastectomy here," she pointed to the scar that had been her right breast. Wendy dropped to her knees, buried her head in Vaughn's lap and began to sob.

Everyone with either a front or a side view witnessed it. Those who did gasped. Whitney was the lone exception. Vaughn Berglund had raised his eyes and lifted his head slightly.

Whitney seized the moment. He helped Wendy to her feet, but his lack of facial expression and formal body language suggested it was merely a next step exercise rather than an act of compassion. Seeing what was happening, Linda rushed to Wendy's side. She helped her to a seat and hugged her.

Whitney, meantime, crouched in front of Vaughn. "Hear me, Berglund," he said loud enough to reach everyone in the room. "Hear me. Did you do it? Did you erase Orrin Burdette and play the *skin flick* on the night of June 19th, 1962? Move your head yes or no. Please, we need closure."

The room fell silent. All that could be heard came from outside – a police car's siren. Every eyeball was on Vaughn Berglund. Those without a direct line of sight scurried for position.

After several seconds, Vaughn moved his head from side-to-side. It was ever so brief a motion; so slight it was done in a blink. But it was a definite no. Whitney's chin sank to his chest and his body became limp.

Most everyone present responded with considerate applause.

"Wow! We all need a drink after that," Reno shouted out. "I'm still buying. How about we switch to tequila poppers? Anybody object?"

Whitney Crawford rose slowly to his feet. Perspiration dripped from his forehead. Sweat pockets appeared under both of his arms. "Don't forget, we still have Penny Sexton to go."

Linda Dalby, shook her head at the mention of Penny. Something in her gut told her Whitney shouldn't go there.

The bartender furiously tried to keep pace with the orders of tequila poppers when police reappeared through the rear exit. Chief McWorter Jr. was again their point man. He asked for Dee Dee Wellborn, who, her hair a mess and her blouse unbuttoned; came running through the main entrance as if she'd been cued. "They went that way," she shouted, pointing in the direction of the parking lot. "They're two old guys."

Everyone's focus was on the cops, except for Scott Clayton. His attention was diverted to another surprise visitor who'd entered the room as the cops were racing out; his dad's right hand man, Enrique Zendejas. "What the hell?" Scott wondered aloud.

"You know him?" Linda said.

"He's worked for my dad for over twenty-five years."

"What would he be doing here?"

"Can't imagine, but he doesn't go to the bathroom without my dad knowing about it."

"Do you like him?"

"I don't like anyone who works for my dad, especially him. He followed me to a crack house once when I was going through my really dark period, and instead of helping me get to rehab, he called the cops on me. I did jail time. Enrique gets screen credits as a location director, but he's really my dad's errand boy. Watch this," Scott said as he walked away.

"*Que paso?*" Scott said, as he approached Enrique. "What's Errand Boy doing in a place like this?"

Enrique's eyebrows snapped up. "*Mi amigo*, I was about to ask you the same. Are you here by invitation?"

"My date is an old classmate of Dad's."

"She have a name?"

"That's for you to find out."

"Which one is she?"

Scott turned and searched out Linda. "The blonde in front of the Bush poster."

"Attractive."

"It goes beyond that."

"Little old for Romeo, no?"

"It's not a factor."

"Serious?"

"I am."

"Does your dad know about her?"

"He will as soon as you report back to him."

"*Touche.*"

"What brings you here, Enrique?"

"A little research for your Dad."

"How so?"

"He's got a screenplay about the *skin flick* incident. Wants to film it on location in Santa Barbara. He's having a time with the police chief over costs to the city. So, he's asked me to recruit some class members to endorse the project. How about your girlfriend? Think she'd volunteer to be a contact?"

"You can ask her. Let me give her a heads up. Here," Scott handed Enrique a ten dollar bill, "get yourself a drink in the meantime."

Linda Dalby listened attentively as Scott briefed her on his conversation with Enrique. "I'd be honored to be at the top of his contact list," Linda said with a wink. "I'll be happy to speak for his project."

"Your name on that list will speak for itself, Linda. Especially when Dad finds out you're with me."

"Wouldn't you love to be a fly on the wall?"

"Knowing my dad it would be a bedroom wall."

CHAPTER 29

"While Dee Dee was preoccupied with assisting the police and Whitney was still licking his wounds from Vaughn Berglund's visceral testimony, Reno took it upon himself to try and inject some life into the party. "Can we break for some music?" he asked everyone. The response was a resounding yes.

"Do you guys know Peppermint Twist?" Reno asked *The Occasion's* vocalist.

"We don't do sixties stuff," the girl said. "None of us were born then."

"Well, how about anything that doesn't sound like a theme for bipolar disorder?"

Reno and his classmates had to settle for a funked-out version of Kenny Loggins' *Footloose*.

Reno asked Holly to dance. She declined at first saying it had been too many years. Reno refused to take no for an answer. He squatted down in front of her chair, pulled her forward by her arms, rolled her up onto his shoulders and carried her to the dance floor.

"Now just shake your booty," he laughed as he lowered her feet to the floor.

"Don't shake yours," Holly smiled. "I doubt this building is earthquake proof."

The two of them traded more insults before the song ended. "Now, you can slow it down," Reno hollered at the musicians.

They accommodated with something vaguely akin to Willie Nelson's *All of Me*.

Reno wasted no time in pressing close to Holly. She didn't protest.

"Some things never change," Reno said.

"What's that?"

"You feel as comfortable in my arms as ever. It's like I swallowed a time capsule."

"You feel pretty good yourself, Reno."

"Think your mother would approve of us dancing tonight?"

"God rest her soul. Are you kidding? The day I broke up with you was the happiest day of her life."

"Spreading joy has been my mission in life."

Reno purposely slid his cheek next to Holly's and waited for any sign of resistance. There was none. They danced that way for two more slow songs. Not saying anything. As soon as the music stopped, they stood facing one another, still holding hands.

"Time out for a smoke?"

"Gave it up years ago, Reno."

"Still do when I'm anxious. Mind if I – "

"Not at all."

"Let's go outside. How about my truck?"

"Sounds like something we did back when."

"My intentions are good."

"I trust you."

Reno stopped by the bar and slammed down another tequila popper on his way out the door with Holly. He smoked a Marlboro while Holly waited in the truck. When he finally joined her he turned on the ignition and popped a Tim McGraw CD in the stereo.

"I played against his dad, Tug, a couple of times in A ball."

"Wasn't he the 'You Gotta Believe' guy?"

"Excellent knowledge, Holly. I'm impressed."

"Don't forget, my dad was big into sports."

Without explanation, Reno suddenly ejected the CD. "Too much of a distraction," he said.

"You want to talk, don't you?"

Reno nodded that he did. "You read my signs well."

"Always could."

"What are your thoughts about tonight, Holly?"

"You want the politically correct version or – "

"You know me better than that."

"You were borderline cruel to Wendy."

"How was I to know she'd had cancer?"

"Breast cancer is detected every two minutes."

"Okay, it was insensitive, but it got Vaughn acquitted. And wait until his sister learns he had a response."

"What have you learned from tonight, Reno?"

"A bunch of people who've had their time in the sun and don't have a tan to show for it."

"That's a little harsh, don't you think?"

"I'm one of 'em." Reno scratched at his goatee. "Remember our class slogan?"

"Can't."

"I do. 'And We Will Be Heard.' Not one person in that room tonight has been heard. I can't speak for all those who aren't here. But, from my experience, most people who have been heard in their lifetime are eager to bask in the recognition that comes with it."

"I haven't been heard, Reno, but it doesn't mean my life was a total waste. "I helped the Lord. Granted, it wasn't what I planned, but…"

"That's more to my point. There's no one in that room who is where they planned to be: Linda Dalby, not in Hollywood, Penny Sexton, not yet a queen, me, not in the Hall of Fame. Dee Dee Wellborn, not the president of anything. Take Jimmy Robertson, the redhead with the buzz cut. He lost an arm in Vietnam; one of those booby-traps. Here he is still wearing a constant scowl and brood-ing about his misfortune. I doubt he planned that in fifty years we'd all be feeling sorry for him."

"You're being too hasty, Reno. "You're making a value judgment based solely on what you've observed tonight. There is always more to the story."

"Maybe. But I see a lot of myself in these people. When I found myself wallowing in the minor leagues and finally acknowledged I wasn't going to make Cooperstown, I knew my life as I had planned it, was over. I remember tripping on some Angel Dust and walking the beach from Santa Barbara to Ventura one night, chanting, 'I won't be heard'. Since the day I took off my uniform for the last time, I've walked through life not really caring if I live another day. I'm not suicidal. Just not terribly interested in what lies ahead. I have no passion for hosting a sports radio show. It's what I do once another day arrives. It's easy. Something I know. That's what I see here tonight…people without a purpose. All it does for me is reinforce the notion of the curse."

"What's your interpretation of the curse, Reno? Does it have a face? Does it speak?"

"Funny you should mention that. When my car broke down on the drive here, I thought, there goes the curse rearing his ugly ahead again." Reno paused to cup his index finger and thumb around the steering wheel and waved his hand across the wheel like it was a magic wand. "My curse is a he. He's ugly as sin. His eyes look like a large bird has clawed them. His face is badly pocked and his beard is long and scraggily. He comes to me as an opposing pitcher. He spits on the ground as he plants his toes on the rubber and then wipes the snot off his nose with the back of his glove. When he finally cranks the ball and fires it at me it breaks into my hands with the speed of a meteor and the bend of a rainbow. I can't get out of the way in time and the ball cracks me on my knuckles, usually dropping me to my knees."

"Pretty real," Holly said.

"What's your curse like?"

"It's a gray cloud that descends over my brain. It disrupts my good thoughts and fills my head with bad ones. And, suddenly it's gone. No good-bye. No nothing."

"If you asked me, yours is scarier. It's not defined."

Holly reached out and grabbed Reno by the hand. "Let's go back inside and make it our purpose to enjoy these people one last time for as long as the party lasts. Okay?"

When they returned, the music was still slow. They danced cheek-to-cheek without saying a word.

As the musicians finished their version of the Eagles' *Take It Easy,* Reno felt fingernails claw into the skin behind his neck, ripping away skin.

"You cheating, son of a bitch!" Reno immediately recognized his assailant's voice: Pearl.

Reno pushed Holly from the line of fire. "I'll explain," he said.

"You'll explain to me," Pearl said, punching Reno in the stomach with a vicious right uppercut.

Reno gasped for air.

"You're not gone twenty-four hours and how do I find you? Liquored-up and resting your lame dick on some 'has been's' cottage cheese thighs." Pearl's complexion had turned the color of her red hair. There was so much anger in her eyes, Reno wondered if they hurt.

"Can we take this outside?" Reno said, trying to grab hold of Pearl's arm. All that got him was a backhand slap on the cheek.

"No we can't," Pearl hollered. "Cause I want every last filthy cunt you ever porked in high school to know that fifty years later you're the king of 'one and done.' Gals this man couldn't get hard twice in one night unless he wrapped his limp dick in a cast."

"Enough," Reno said, taking her arm with more force this time. Quickly he moved the two of them in the direction of the back exit.

That only infuriated Pearl more. She pulled herself free, stepped back and karate kicked Reno so hard in the chest that he fell backwards, landing square on his ass.

"That old gray mare you're dancin' with," Pearl snorted, "looks like she's been rode from New Mexico to here without rest. Ought to take her to a large animal vet and get her checked out."

Just then, Lance Vance and his cameraman approached Reno. Lance again turned his back to the action to face the camera. "Rolling?" he asked his cameraman.

"Speed."

"This domestic dispute that's raging uncontrollably behind me," Lance began, "is another example of the chaos that has characterized this first San Marcos class of '62 reunion in a half century. I'm Lance Vance. I'll have the details live at eleven."

Reno waited for Lance to finish before he got to his feet. "Is that a wrap, TV man?"

Lance ignored him, telling his cameraman to "Spray the place."

Reno turned to Pearl. "You're going out of here if I have to knock you silly."

"That won't be necessary," a voice blasted over a police bullhorn, the sound ricocheting off the activity center's walls. It was Chief McWorter Jr. His ominous presence however, didn't stop Pearl from punching Reno again, this time in the ribs.

"I've got my hands full right now with a pair of thieves," the chief spoke into the mouthpiece, "but if I find this ruckus still going on when I'm finished, I'll shut this dog and pony show down for another fifty years."

CHAPTER 30

Dee Dee Wellborn was still seething over Mustafa Muhammad's cowardice when she finally caught up with the three police officers who'd chased Vernon and Cecil down an alley, across a playground and into the kitchen of a recently opened KFC.

She was out of breath and her legs were fatigued, which she attributed more to riding Mustafa's wide rail than the running required in tracking down the cops.

"Have you got them?" Dee Dee asked the cop who seemed to be in charge, a big, raw-boned man in his late fifties who had a snowy white handlebar moustache and wore sunglasses in the dark.

"We've made contact with someone in the store who has confirmed it's them."

"Two old farts, right, officer..."

"Patterson. Sergeant Irv Patterson." He gestured to the others. "That's Officer Klimkoch and Officer Marichal."

"Pleased to meet you," Dee Dee said, trying to finish buttoning her blouse.

"To answer your question, we think by the way they waddled they're either old farts or have hemorrhoid problems; or both. We damn near caught up to them from two blocks away and none of us is a threat to make the Olympic team."

"That's funny," Dee Dee said. "I always thought cops had to undergo humor removal surgery in order to join the force."

"You've seen way too many cop shows," Officer Klimkoch said.

"So, let's go get 'em," Dee Dee said.

"Not so fast," Sergeant Patterson said. "We think we may have a hostage situation."

"What are they using to hold people hostage, drumsticks?" Dee Dee said. She prided herself on her quick wit.

"You're the funny one," the sergeant said with a smile.

Officer Marichal's cell phone rang. He was appointed the contact, because the caller didn't speak English. Officer Marichal listened for maybe thirty seconds and then told the caller "*Esperate.*" He dutifully reported what he'd learned. "There are two workers being held. They say all the old guys want is their van from the Sea Breeze parking lot and a ten minute head start."

"Seriously, what kind of weapons do they have that they could hold anyone hostage?"

"Golf clubs," Officer Marichal answered. "A pair of jumbo drivers."

✡ ✡ ✡

Cecil attempted to straighten the part in his hair without benefit of a mirror. He always strived to look like a professional crook. "How can somebody work in a fast food place," Cecil said, looking directly at the hostage who called himself Raul, "if they can't speak English?"

"Shit, Cecil, haven't you ever ordered from a drive-up?" Vernon chimed in. "None of them speak English. It's why when you order a Whopper and fries, you get fish sticks and onion rings."

"How do we know they told the cops what we wanted, Vernon?"

"Because I heard him say 'van',"

Raul and his hostage mate smiled at one another.

"While we've got this Mexican stand-off going," Vernon said, "why don't you take what's in the cash registers, Cecil?"

"Cause theft is a felony, Vernon."

"Well, what do you think we're facing right now, misdemeanor disturbing the peace charges?"

"Hey, Vernon. I told you we didn't break and enter at the Sea Breeze. And, a good lawyer will get us past charges of voyeurism. And, as far as I'm concerned, we just stopped in this place to use the restroom and have someone pick up our van for us; kinda like valet parking. We're still golden, Vernon. But, not if we take money."

"Fuck, Cecil. You've already eaten a nine-piece box of crispy dark meat. That's the same as stealing."

"So, we'll tell the cops Raul, gave it to some friends who showed up at the back door. That's the way Mexicans are. They steal for all their relatives, not just themselves like us."

The kitchen phone rang again. Raul answered. *"Como esta. Que paso?* Raul listened attentively for a minute and then said, *"Esperate, todos noches."*

"I'm pretty sure that means they're going along with all our demands, Cecil. T*odos* means all."

"I don't know, Vernon. I just don't trust someone I can't understand. Not when our asses are on the line."

✵ ✵ ✵

Dee Dee placed her hands on her hips and held her chin high. "Sergeant Patterson, I don't care what tactics you use. I've got a party I'm missing and I'm not going to wait around on these farts any longer."

"What are you planning to do, Ms…?"

"Wellborn."

"We can't risk those hostages getting hurt."

"I'm going to walk in the front door, place an order for a chicken twister and then bust into the kitchen and grab those two old farts by the balls and drag them out to the street. Those men had the indecency to spy on me while I was, you know…and I want them hung by their nuts."

"I can't let you do that, Ms. Wellborn," Sergeant Patterson said.

"Try and stop me." Dee Dee started to walk away from the mini-command post the cops had set up, only to have Sergeant Patterson catch up to her, wrap one of his long arms around her waist, lift her off the ground, carry her toward an arriving squad car and dispatch her head first into the back seat.

"You wait here Ms. Dee Dee," the sergeant said.

"For a man as strong as you," Dee Dee said with a smile, "I'll wait 'till I'm too old to remember what I'm waiting on."

✳ ✳ ✳

Vernon told Cecil to check out the counter in case the cops had the front of the store staked out.

"Business as usual," Vernon reported back after being gone only a few seconds. "There's a homeless guy smoking filters at a corner table and a large black woman with five kids who's hacked off because her twenty-piece box didn't have enough crispy thighs."

Shortly after Cecil returned to the kitchen, Raul entertained a notion. "You pay me and Julio cash and we'll get you out of here safely."

"What happened to the Spanish?" Cecil said, suddenly sporting an "I told you so" look on his face.

"Yeah, what gives?" Vernon said.

"When it involves the cops I always speak Spanish first," Raul said.

Vernon put his hand to his chin and began to pace despite the fact there was very little room in the kitchen. "You want us, the hostage takers, to pay you the hostages. What's wrong with this picture, Cecil?"

"The longer we stay here the less the chances they'll bring us our van."

"They're not bringing your van. What you heard me say was '*Viene cuando estes listo. Te ayudaremos.*' It means come here when you're ready. We'll help you. You heard *viene* and thought it was van.

"I told you, Vernon."

"Okay. Okay!" Vernon pointed his finger at Raul's chest. "How you gonna get us out of here?"

"The Pepsi guy is due here any minute with his delivery. The guy is like clockwork. He's been training a guy all week, so there will be two of them. We put you guys in their uniforms and you walk out of here like nothing ever happened."

"What's it going to cost us? Cecil asked.

"Your drivers," Raul said.

"How do you know the Pepsi guys will go along with the idea?" Vernon said.

"We'll split what we get for the drivers with them. It's better money than they make in a day in that shit job. Besides, if you steal their truck they won't have to work the rest of the night. Don't worry. I'll work everything out."

"If you slice off the tee, this is the perfect club for you" Cecil said, handing over his *Power Stroke* to Julio.

Just as Raul had advertised, the Pepsi guys showed up on time and went along with the program. Vernon and Cecil giggled like a couple of teenagers as they backed the delivery truck out of the driveway and sped off toward who knew where.

"We're lucky to have survived that one, Vernon."

"We're not out of the woods yet."

"You could fool me."

162

"We're out of gas, Cecil."

"Shit!"

"Shit is right. Who isn't going to be suspicious of two old guys sitting in a stalled out Pepsi truck? What do we say, 'Just waiting for Triple *A*'?"

"I see your point, Vernon."

CHAPTER 31

Even though he was only six months out of Stanford and a reporter for just over half of that time, Lance Vance had already earned the distinction of being the lead reporter on KEUR-TV-Eureka's three person staff, meaning whatever the day's top story was, he was assigned to cover it. Lance's five-part investigative series exposing an inordinate number of police brutality complaints against the Eureka P.D. that lacked any administrative follow-up, had vaulted him to the head of the class.

"You just don't find good aggressive journalism in a market this size," news director Randal Edmonds was quoted as saying in the *Humboldt Times*. "Lance is a real tiger."

His first assignment as the lead reporter was President Reagan's first visit to the Redwood Empire since he'd campaigned for governor.

That's not to say Lance didn't encounter a few speed bumps on his way to prominence. In his second week on the job he was assigned to interview a Bank of America official for a story about skyrocketing interests rates and how they were impacting the local economy. While he was doing the interview, two guys robbed the bank and made off with fifty thousand dollars. Lance rightfully abandoned the story he was working on and had his cameraman shoot the bank interior and exterior. He did an interview with the bank manager focusing on the security breach. But when he returned to the TV station to put his story together Edmonds asked why he hadn't interviewed any of the half-dozen or more eyewitnesses.

"I saw the holdup," Lance told his boss. "Who better to give a first-hand account? Why waste tape on the average bystander?"

Randal Edmonds, who, despite considerable resistance from Janet Nyborg, had directed Lance to change his last name from Nyborg to Vance before he started work at KEUR, evoked the name Geraldo Rivera in a newsroom dressing down about the significance of the reporter never becoming bigger than the story.

Because of the fallout from the police brutality series, Lance was subsequently forced to tiptoe around the halls of the police department in his daily search for stories. His sources within the department, which he'd worked tirelessly to establish, had all but dried up over night. "You screwed with Blue," was the message.

Through it all, Lance was unwaveringly bold and eager to advance to a bigger market and bigger money. Through a reliable campus security source at College of the Redwoods, Lance had gotten wind of an arrest by Eureka P.D. of what was said to be the central figure in a steroid black market ring that was targeting students – mostly the school's jocks.

"He's an itinerant surfer," Lance's source told him over coffee at the Java Farm, located just a block from campus. "Goes by the name of Wayne Preston. He's forty-four, dark tan, goofy blonde hair. He's been living in an abandoned trailer about a half-mile up from campus."

"How does he support himself?" Lance asked his contact.

"Handyman stuff."

"What are the charges?"

"Operating a muscle juice ring."

"Heavy stuff."

"Word is, the evidence is thin."

"You say he's out on bail."

"Yesterday."

"Can you hook me up with this Preston guy?"

"I'll try."

"There are a couple of Andrew Jacksons in it for you."

"Always happy to serve."

Lance smiled at the remark.

It's hard to figure where Lance got his professional aggressiveness. Growing up as the only child of an unwed mother, he didn't demonstrate any of those tendencies.

Perhaps because there was no dominant male in his life – his grandfather, Joe Nyborg, preferred stamp collecting to boy activities, like baseball and Boy Scouts – Lance was borderline timid. He played basketball in high school but even though he had good size at 6'4", he was always the last player off the bench. "The Swede from Weed" his teammates would call him when they wanted to mock his robot-like footwork under the basket. A natural he was not.

It wasn't until he was assigned to give the valedictory address at graduation from Weed that Lance found something that interested him – a microphone, and the power it possessed. His five-minute speech, which centered on developing a sense of community, drew rave reviews from such lofty places as the superintendent's office.

"Look beyond your self-interests to the needs of your community," he'd said, "lest you be abandoned by the community's ability to service your best interests."

Six months before his graduation from Weed High, Janet Nyborg rewarded her son with the then seventy thousand plus dollars, insisting that he use it toward a Stanford education. Lance wanted to know how she'd managed to save that kind of money on a telephone installer's pay. Janet wouldn't tell him and eventually he quit asking. Lance used the money wisely, graduating from Stanford's broadcast journalism school with honors.

Acting through Lance's source, Preston had agreed to meet at a picnic area in Cedar Grove, a Redwood State Park about fifteen miles south of Eureka. However when Lance and his cameraman arrived, Preston told them the deal was off. He proclaimed his innocence off camera, but he refused to do the interview. He claimed he'd been set up by a Eureka cop. He said it was the cop's revenge for catching him having an affair with his wife.

"Sorry man," Preston said. "I hadn't planned on stiffing you, but the heat is too intense right now."

Lance, the lead reporter had come up empty. There would be no as advertised "exclusive talk with an accused drug peddler" on the six o'clock news. Lance was shaken by the embarrassment of a blown scoop. In the days after Lance promised himself no one would ever professionally use and abuse him again.

CHAPTER 32

Cha Cha Miranda banged the office door behind her so hard many of the diners stopped eating to look in her direction.

"*Todo esta bien*," she said, waving her exposed palms in opposite directions. Her assurances to the contrary, Cha Cha was not in a good mood. Regulars understood she was given to displays of temper and paid her no matter. Cha Cha was justified, however, for feeling a bit stretched. Her dishwasher of a week was a "no show," she'd had to perform the Heimlich maneuver on a drunken technology salesman when a tortilla chip went down wrong, and she was having an awful time finding a replacement for Frederico Romo, the legendary "Guitar Man" who'd been a weekend night fixture at her restaurant for twenty-five years. To top it off, the morning paper was full of bad news about the economy.

Tourism was off fifteen percent again this summer according to the article; not that she needed to read it in the paper to know. Casa de Cha Cha was going through a rough spell. She'd been at the same location for so many years she'd become immune to panic over a downward turn in the economy, but when you threw in the other, it made for a sullen Cha Cha Miranda.

Plus, she was tired. She'd only recently recognized that thirty-five years of twelve to fourteen hour days, six days a week managing Casa de Cha Cha was making for lines on her neck and face with greater frequency. Occasionally she'd remark to friends that she was getting to look more like the old Aztec women depicted in the many paintings that adorned her restaurant's walls. What happened to the cute and saucy Mexican salsa queen, she wondered as she studied her reflection in a semi-lit Corona display behind the bar. Maybe what she needed was a man. If not a lover, then at least one to help with the restaurant.

Cha Cha's one great love was a twenty-year affair. Her relationship with Carl Richter was characterized by varying degrees of tenderness and turbulence. Their passion made for sweet music, but too often a bad chord would be struck and lead to periods of intense and prolonged anger and even estrangement.

Cha Cha met Carl, a strapping former amateur rugby player, when he booked Casa de Cha Cha for a party celebrating his fifth wedding anniversary to the loathsome Stella Richter, pampered daughter of State Senator, philanthropist and star polo player, Ewing Spencer. Carl was a hotshot commercial developer with political aspirations. He eventually served two terms as the city's mayor. Somehow, for most of the twenty years, they'd managed to keep their relationship quiet. Only occasionally would they risk being seen together in Santa Barbara. They managed to reserve two weeks a year together at various rendezvous sites along the Baja Peninsula. The vacations and the relationship finally ended when Cha Cha and Carl literally bumped into to Stella and a female in the airport terminal at San Jose del Cabo. Stella had just arrived while Cha Cha and Carl – arm-in-arm – were departing.

Stella was so enraged she pulled a handgun from her purse but Carl was able to wrestle it away from her. Stella's rage was such that Mexican officials detained her departure for a week for her own safety.

When she returned home, Stella threatened to expose Carl's philandering, which surely would have struck a lethal blow to his recently announced candidacy for the State Assembly.

Like any politician worth his salt, Carl, resorted to damage control and broke off the relationship. Cha Cha was so upset by Carl's lack of allegiance she took a half-dozen bags of tortilla chips, crushed them, and then poured them in the tank of his fifty-foot Sea Ray Sundancer power boat. When Carl finally discovered why his engine wouldn't turn over minutes prior to embarking on a weekend "patch it up with Stella" cruise to Santa Catalina, he went ballistic. He contacted the Coast Guard and demanded they arrest Cha Cha and charge her with sabotage. When the Coast Guard balked over an absence of evidence, he went to the local ABC with a tip that Casa de Cha Cha was in the habit of serving alcohol to minors. The director, a longtime customer of Cha Cha's laughed at the notion saying, "Cha Cha's place is cleaner than driven snow."

What appeared on the restaurant's lone TV, situated above and behind the bar didn't help Cha Cha's aggravated state. It was Lance Vance teasing the class of '62 reunion story from the Sea Breeze motel.

"Silencio!" she said to her bartender. *"Este es importante!"*

Cha Cha recognized Lance, not from his TV work – she seldom paid attention to the news – but because he was a regular customer. He'd come in at least once a week for dinner after the early news. She was always surprised by how many margaritas he'd drink for a guy who didn't get off work until eleven thirty.

Until seeing Lance Vance on her TV, Cha Cha had successfully closed her mind to the reunion. She'd read a preview story in the newspaper a month ago, but had subsequently staged a personal boycott of the local media. Seeing Lance Vance's news tease, however, brought it all back. It set in motion the pangs of guilt she'd kept stowed in the far reaches of her mind for all these many years.

CHAPTER 33

Zeke Clayton was still feeling the frustration of dropping his afternoon golf game to the "film commission fuck." His insides were still knotted up, the result of losing. He didn't like to lose a coin flip, let alone a round of golf; even when he gave a stroke a hole.

Lonnie was his convenient, and of late, constant release. After dinner with the chief and his wife, he'd returned with her to his hotel suite and begun another round of no holds barred sex, which, in Zeke's mind, often came perilously close to requiring officials in striped shirts so that no one got hurt.

The sex was temporarily interrupted by a call from Chief McWorter, Jr. The conversation consisted mostly of Zeke saying, "okay." When he finally hung up, Zeke apologized to Lonnie for "going soft on the chief's request. "He wants you to meet him tonight at a little bungalow just up the road from the old Mira Mar in Montecito. He claims use of the place is one of the perks of being the police chief. Probably belongs to some rich fucking gun runner who wants to make sure the chief looks the other way in case shit happens." Zeke Clayton stopped to run his tongue freely over Lonnie's standing-at-attention nipples. The exercise never failed to boost her resting RPMs.

"But you made him the offer only hours ago," Lonnie said. She was on her knees, saddling Zeke's chest, offering him first one breast than the other. She kept her eyes closed, even when she talked.

"Kid in a candy store, is all I can figure. He must have been thinking about your tits ever since he left the restaurant. I can't blame him. You saw the little lady."

"Sure did.'

"A double bagger if ever there was one."

"That's cruel."

"That's a fact."

Lonnie leaned to one side and eased off Zeke's chest and onto her back. She reached across him and began lightly fingering his piece. It was her way of keeping his fire lit while she contemplated the bluntness of his comments.

"I'm not going to like sharing you," Zeke said, his hand roaming Lonnie's inner thigh.

"It's why I'm here. It's part of the job I signed on for."

"Maybe it's that I don't like handing you over to a fucking cop."

"I think you just realized you'll have to rely on your hand when I'm not around."

"You're cocky, Lonnie."

"Speaking of which, bring that bad boy of yours over here."

Zeke started to shift his body closer than abruptly stopped. "Holy Shit!" He shot up so quickly from the bed it made him momentarily dizzy.

"What did I do?" Lonnie said, between short breaths. Her eyes were glazed.

"The TV," Zeke said, pointing at the screen. "It's Scott. He 's talking with a reporter. It looks like he's at that fucking reunion."

"Are you sure?"

"Positive. I'd know that mug anywhere. I figure its cost me about twenty million over the years."

"Was he that bad of an actor?"

"He was that bad at everything."

"So what if he's at a reunion? Everybody has to be someplace."

"Why on God's earth would he be there?" Zeke leaped off the bed and grabbed the silk robe he'd draped over the bathroom door of his one thousand dollar a night Biltmore suite. It signaled the end of sex with Lonnie.

Before Zeke could speculate any more about Scott's motives, his cell phone rang. It was Enrique Zendejas.

"It's old news, Enrique. I know Scott's there," Zeke said, repeatedly running his hand through his thick silver hair. "I just saw him on TV. It was a promo for the eleven o'clock news. Did you talk to him?"

"He sparred with me," Enrique said. "It's not like we're long lost pals."

"You don't suppose he's trying to steal my film idea?"

"He had a date."

"Shit! Anyone there is almost twice his age. Did he give you a name?"

Zeke could hear Enrique fumbling with a paper.

"Linda. Linda Dalby is her name. Ring a bell?"

Zeke could feel his jaw sink. He pulled his cell away from his ear and studied it as if he didn't believe what he'd heard.

"I want you to meet me at that motel in thirty minutes, Enrique."

"I may have worn out my welcome with some of those people, boss."

"We're not going to need an invitation. Follow me, Enrique?"

"If ever there was one person on this planet who'd bend over backwards to screw me, besides my son, it would be Linda Dalby. And, they're fucking dating! A fucking coincidence, you ask? I doubt it. Zeke's face burned bright red. Without warning he hurled his cell phone at the TV. The phones batteries ejected at impact, angering Zeke even more. He grabbed a cocktail glass from the nightstand and hurled it at the wall, shattering glass in every direction. Without a word, Lonnie tiptoed into the adjoining living room.

CHAPTER 34

Penny Sexton was so surprised to have received an invitation in the mail to a class reunion that she had to read it several times. Before finally putting it away she'd made up her mind to attend. She viewed it as a golden opportunity to once and for all get the homecoming queen thing off her chest. She'd have to swap shifts with a co-worker in order to be free on a Saturday night, but several who worked along side her at Rusty's Pizza, owed her a favor.

Penny filed the invitation where she kept all of her personal treasures, in her diary. She regarded the leather bound diary as her link to a "so-called" life. Each time she contributed material to it she'd select a section to re-read. "A trip down memory lane," is how she referred to it. This night, over a bottle and a half of Stone Ridge Merlot, she re-visited her notes and mementos from the ten-year period following high school. It wasn't her favorite time, but then again, what was?

By 1972 Penny had been out of school ten years and still hadn't settled on a man or a career. Worse, she'd never had a steady date or held a steady job. How, she'd often asked herself, could the girl voted "best personality" by her senior classmates, be captive to such mediocrity? Had to be the curse. It wasn't as if her charm and good looks – she was voted among the "elite eight" senior babes by the student editor of the school paper – had gone south on her. At one time or another Penny had trained as a beautician, checked groceries, groomed pets, worked as a receptionist for a law firm, pedaled Mary Kay products, sold shoes, sold flowers, and came very close to selling her body when she was be threatened with eviction by her landlord for falling three months behind on rent.

Rather than sell herself on the street, Penny seized an "out-of-the-blue" opportunity to sell herself to a well-positioned older man. She referred to the match-up as her lay-away arrangement.

It was a week before Christmas 1972. Watergate had happened, McCartney and Wings was becoming increasingly harder to swallow and the Dolphins were on their way to the only undefeated season in NFL history. Penny was invited to the KEYT Christmas party by a friend. Her name was Janie Lassitich. She was a member of the station's staff. Janie had promised Penny a job interview for a vacancy in her public affairs department and wanted her to get a feel for the people in the company. Did she ever.

"And, who do we have here?" Judge Winston Garland asked Janie. Either he didn't realize he'd interrupted their conversation or he didn't care. Penny couldn't decide which.

"Penny Sexton," Janie said. "She's applied for the job as my assistant. Penny, this is Judge Garland. He's one of the owners."

"I'm the only owner that matters," the judge said, popping out his chest in jest. "Pleased to meet you," Penny said, flashing her best Pepsodent smile. "It's a great party. Your employees are so…nice. That's the best word I can think of."

"You'll have to do better as a wordsmith if you're going to work here. This is, after all, a communication business," the judge said, exhibiting a playful grin.

In the years since he'd married Edna, the judge had established a reputation as a power drinker – primarily vodka martinis. It was apparent to Penny that Judge Garland had downed a healthy portion of his own cheer before he'd moved in on her conversation with Janie. His eyes were sunset red and on occasion he'd rock forward as if he was struggling with his balance.

Penny didn't think much of it when the judge said to Janie in parting, "Make sure this attractive young lady sees me in my office before she interviews with the station manager."

The meeting with Judge Garland took place four days later. Penny had squeezed her extremely tight budget by buying a wool business suit for the occasion. The judge greeted Penny in his office with an enthusiastic handshake then a surprise hug, which he held for a considerable time, long enough for Penny to be able to identify his cologne as Old Spice. She considered his dress to be casually elegant for a man rumored to be in his late seventies. He wore a gray herringbone jacket with a black silk shirt, open at the neck.

Judge Garland's office was spacious with scenic views of the city from two large picture windows. After greeting Penny he took a seat behind a massive walnut desk. The desk, as with everything it his office was free of clutter. It looked to Penny like a movie set piece rather than a working office.

"A little starter beverage for you, Ms. Sexton," the judge said, as he turned and opened a small refrigerator behind his desk. "Care for a chilled Chardonnay? As you can see," he pointed to a half-empty glass resting next to the telephone, "I started without you."

"I probably shouldn't," Penny replied. "I want to make a good impression on Mr. Steiner when he interviews me."

"Mr. Steiner does what he's told," the judge smiled, his lip turning up, and indication he was pleased with the way the conversation was going. "That's another way of saying, if I tell him to hire you, he will."

"Well," Penny blushed ever so slightly, "let's hope that's the message he receives."

"It will be, if..." The judge paused for effect.

Penny had not expected what was coming.

"If you join me for a romantic weekend in Lake Tahoe at the beginning of the new year."

Against her better judgment, Penny did. She so pleased the judge that a week after their return, she hopscotched over Janie, replacing her as public affairs director at twice her salary.

Over the next seven months, the judge and Penny rendezvoused monthly in such adventurous locations as Beaver Creek, Park City, Palm Springs, Hilton Head, Cabo San Lucas, Nuevo Vallarta and Princeville at Kaui,

During a weeklong stay at the Grand Melia in Cabo San Lucas, Judge Garland shocked Penny with a proposition that was so vile she hopped a plane for home and never spoke with him again.

He had returned to their suite after practicing snorkeling in the Grand Melia's giant pool. They were scheduled for a snorkeling expedition the following day with several other guests of the hotel. Penny was glad she'd suggested the activity; it would mean a much-needed break from sex with the judge. Penny had grown weary of their extended bouts of sex. It took the judge so long to get off each time that, after four days, she was approaching terminal boredom. She figured the boat ride to and from the lagoon plus the snorkeling and a goodly amount of tequila would provide her at least a twenty-four hour respite.

"Let's talk," the judge said to Penny, who'd just finished putting on her turquoise bikini and was in the middle of coating her entire body with sun block. Talking was not one of the judge's attributes on these getaways, except when he was angling for sex, so Penny was a little surprised by the suggestion.

"How much do you love me?"

Penny squirmed ever so slightly on the make-up bench she was sitting on. She could feel her lips go dry. The "L" word had never come up in conversation in the nearly seven months they'd been sneaking off together.

"I love being with you very much, Judge."

"We shouldn't have to hide our love," the judge said, looking out the window at a distant fishing boat.

Penny didn't know where this talk was going but she wished it could have waited. For the first time she felt very uncomfortable in the judge's presence. She'd never seen him "out there" before. His eyes appeared to pop out of their sockets.

"Why don't we just get rid of Edna and enjoy each other without the hassle of trying to keep it a secret. I've figured out how I can keep most of her money."

Penny's eyebrows nearly came in contact with her hairline. "Are we talking murder?" Penny could hear her voice crack.

"She's not going away on her own anytime soon. The woman is so fit from all her walking. She'll live into the next century. Mark my word."

Penny got off the bench and walked to the couch in the center of the three-room suite and slowly sat down. Her glazed eyes reflected her astonishment. "How could you even dream of such an idea? The thought of killing someone is repulsive to me." Penny swallowed heavily.

The judge's face turned red. He raised his voice considerably. "I can implicate you without you participating," he smiled, his lip turning up in one corner.

"Don't flatter yourself, your Honor. You're not that smart."

"Smart enough to know everything about you and the many jobs you held before joining my public affairs department." The judge fumbled with his robe before putting it on over his wet swim shorts. "Smart enough to know that in every job you held, only two of which you listed on your resume, you had a personality clash with your manager or supervisor that bordered on physical confrontation. Want to tell me about the veterinarian who you called a bitch and threatened with a pair of scissors because she caught you being 'overly aggressive' with animals that were boarding at her clinic?"

Penny fell against the back of the couch. Her eyes were wide, her heart racing. How did he know so much about her?

"Don't tell me violence repulses you."

"You disgust me," Penny said, slamming her fist into the arm of the couch and then leaping to her feet. She would later understand that her aggressiveness was a reflection of both her anger and her fear.

"I will not be a party to murder," Penny said, moving in the direction of the bedroom. "Surely, you must be joking."

"Not in the least," the judge said.

"I'm taking the first plane out of here," Penny announced.

The judge caught her at the entrance to the bedroom closet. His eyes were red with rage, or was it the chlorine, Penny wondered. "You're not leaving me, Penny. Not ever." He pulled both hands free from his bathrobe pockets, placed them around her neck and began to squeeze.

Penny acted quickly. She brought both arms up, slamming them into the judge's extended arms with such force that he loosened his grip. As the judge struggled with his balance from the blow, Penny planted a knee so hard into his groin she half expected to see her kneecap come out his rectum. The judge crumpled to the floor then flopped onto his back like a performing seal. He moaned as if he'd been shot, which he would have been if Penny hadn't left her gun at home.

"You tell Edna anything about us and I'll have you killed," were the judge's last words to Penny.

Penny made it home safely and by the following day was back looking for job opportunities at the local employment office. Better she was again in need of work, she reasoned, than working off time making license plates.

CHAPTER 35

It had been twenty minutes since Penny had retired to a chair in the corner of the activity center. She was far removed from any of the hard partying. She'd immersed herself in private thoughts, not to mention several white Russians, which she'd lined up on the floor next to her feet. She stared at her shoes as others danced to The Occasions and compared bad things that had happened to their lives. That's what Penny assumed they were doing. Why else would they all be shaking their heads and looking so terribly depressed?

"Shit!" Penny said, not loud enough for anyone to hear over the music. She could see Whitney Crawford preparing to cross-examine her. Too bad he's never going to have the chance, she told herself. He'd taken his center-circle seat and was reviewing notes. God, she hated him as much now as she did in high school. He was always arguing with teachers in class because he was on the debate team and wanted to show off. No, she hated him more now.

She hated Reno Parris, then and now, too. She could see him holding court at the bar where he'd been most of the night, laughing at life. Reno, of all people, she reasoned, had no business laughing at anything from all she'd heard that had gone wrong in his life. But there he was, yucking it up as always. Pig! It was Reno who'd fucked her in the worst way possible all those years ago, just because she wouldn't let him bonk her – his words. If she'd had it to do over again she would have accepted his uninspiring, unprotected dick and given him change back.

Then there was Linda Dalby. How positively vulgar she looked dancing with a guy young enough to be her son. Probably big Yanni fans, Penny laughed. God, she dances the same way she always did, like she was trying to read book titles off library shelves; all the sensuality of a sea turtle. What was it guys saw in her? And what was up with her date? Are all the women his age taken? There's a red flair, she mused.

Whitney Crawford's voice coming from a speaker that was positioned too close to her head, jolted Penny's wandering mind. She checked her watch to help herself get reoriented. It was 10:50PM. That meant she'd been drinking for almost six hours, counting the rum-and-something concoctions she'd made at home before coming to the Sea Breeze.

"Will Penny Sexton please come forward," Whitney said. There was a smattering of applause.

By now Penny had retrieved a second chair for her feet and was halfway lying down. "Come and get me," Penny hollered. "I've had too many white Russians. Those little Commie bastards pack a wallop. Come to think about it, they're not communists any more. Ah, the world is a better place because of it. Fear not the white Russians any more." Penny dropped her head toward her chest for a second, as if to re-energize herself. "With all the cops coming in and out of this place, I'm afraid of getting a DUI, or would it be a WUI? There isn't a breathalyzer on this planet that would let me skate."

Whitney answered Penny's call, placing his microphone on a chair and limping noticeably to where she was sitting. Penny could tell by his eyes that Whitney had been drinking. She correctly figured that the interrogation of Vaughn Berglund had taken its toll on him.

"Such a gentleman," Penny said, offering her arm to Whitney. He guided her to the chair opposite his and called for everyone to take their seats.

It took longer this time for everyone to settle. Penny figured it was the booze slowing everyone's reaction time.

"I must begin by stating that Sexton is the last classmate to be cross-examined," Whitney said. His cheek muscles twitched, he was so tense. "If she can account for her actions on that fateful night, then we're all...well, we're fucked. Fucked again. Because we'll be back to square one, unable to finger who did it; unable to once and for all appease a community that hates our collective guts. More important, the curse will continue."

"Excuse me, your fucking honor, or whatever you are." Penny said. "But you're pre-judging me and my peers."

"Prejudicing?"

"Have it your way, Whitney."

"What would you like, for me to confess so we'll all be free of the curse and we can really get down to some serious drinking?"

"Do what feels right, girl," Reno Parris shouted from the bar.

"Fuck yourself, Reno," Penny said, flipping him off. "You're such a disgusting piece of – "

"Can we proceed?" Whitney said.

"Hey," Reno shot back. "You and Penny can turn cartwheels for all I fuckin' care."

At the mention of cartwheels, Penny got out of her chair, cleared some space around the perimeter of the inner circle and started performing them; first in one direction, then the other. One of The Occasions played a monkey grinder tune on the keyboard. Despite all the liquor she'd consumed, her execution was flawless. Penny had easily been the most athletic of the school's cheerleaders and she wasn't leaving any doubt that she still had it.

Before Penny stopped her routine, Lance Vance and his cameraman, Skip who, without Dee Dee around, were camping on the steps to the activity center entrance, re-entered on the run. Lance told his guy to roll and roll he did, dropping to the floor near Penny for some provocative low angle shots. Moments after Penny finally stopped because of dizziness, Lance Vance hollered at his cameraman, "We're hot in ten seconds."

"Ready!"

"Thanks Rita," Lance said, breaking into a fake smile as he addressed the camera. "We are live at the Sea Breeze motel where a small number of members of San Marcos High's class of '62 have gathered for a first: a class reunion." Lance signaled for Skip to pan the activity center. "That's right. It's the first time they've gathered in fifty years and as you can see they're getting a little rowdy."

Upset by being upstaged, but rational enough to recognize a golden opportunity, Penny made her way to where

Lance was talking and pulled at his arm. "I have something I want to say."

Lance did his best to ignore her. "We spoke with some of the returning class members during a break in the activities, and here's what they had to say about a reputed curse on the class of '62."

Lance dropped his microphone to his side, and listened through his earpiece as each of those he'd interviewed appeared on pre-recorded tape.

"Are you going to interview me?" Penny shouted, apparently thinking Lance's earpiece was a hearing aid.

"Somebody get her away from me." Lance pulled his arm free of Penny's grip.

"We're back live again. It should be pointed out," Lance said, again talking directly into the camera, "that already two class members have been questioned about their activity that – "

"And, I'm the third," Penny said, the camera still showing only Lance. "But, if you don't mind I'd like to say something to the nice people in your audience."

Lance demonstrated his coolness under pressure by continuing his live hit without being distracted. "Both were grilled at length – "

"If you're going to interrupt my cross…whatever, than for God sakes, interview me," Penny said, again pulling at Lance's arm. "Here," she said reaching as if to take control of Lance's hand microphone, "let me introduce myself."

At this point the director back at Channel Three's studio was forced to include Penny in the shot. He instructed Skip to do so. Aware of the fact, Lance stepped toward the camera. "You'll excuse the interruptions. Rita, I'd like to take a short break while I clear up some logistical problems at this end."

"Sure thing, Lance. Just give us a thumbs up when you're ready to resume. Just a suggestion, you might want to 'deep six' the woman who is acting like your shadow."

"Consider it done, Rita."

Lance dropped his microphone to his side as soon as the tally light on the camera went off, then turned and faced Penny. "Get the fuck out of my shot, will you lady. I'm trying to do my job and you're interfering. Don't you have a date you can suffocate with your self-absorbtion?"

Penny's face turned day-glow red, which somehow seemed to make her freckles multiply. She abruptly spun around and stomped off toward the corner chair she'd been sitting in most of the evening.

Meantime, Lance signaled it was safe to return live to the Sea Breeze. "Thanks again, Rita," he said. "As I was saying..."

Just as he'd started to talk Penny returned and without saying a word jabbed the pointed end of a pair of scissors she'd found in her purse into Lance's neck, then quickly retracted it. Again, the director was left no option other than to have Skip include Penny in the picture. Blood spit from Lance's wound almost immediately. He tried his best not to acknowledge the attack. He placed his free hand to the wound and continued. "Thus far there have been two acquittals in this makeshift court of scant legitimacy."

Penny, who'd escaped a vigorous attempt by Reno to restrain her by scratching his nose with a nail, approached Lance again. This time, rather that stab at him, she positioned the sharp end against his jugular. "Let me talk or I will rip you a place to store your chin," Penny said, her eyes darting nervously from the camera to Lance and back.

With the pain of his wound now exceeding his adrenalin flow, Lance nodded in compliance.

"Hold the microphone toward my mouth and keep quiet," Penny said, pressuring the scissors just enough to break his skin once more. "And make sure your cameraman moves to his left so he gets my good side. Is that understood?"

"Everyone hears you," Lance said like someone who'd swallowed a spoon.

Penny brought her left hand up to where she had the scissors parked against Lance's jugular and quickly switched hands, never allowing the sharp point to stray from contact. Now she could take the microphone in her right hand and speak from a more natural position.

"First of all, I'm Penny Sexton and I'm damn proud to be a member of the class of '62, even though my life has been ruined by it." She felt Lance try to lean away from her so she pushed against him immediately, never allowing the sharp point of the scissors to lift off his flesh. "But, I don't want to talk about who put the *skin flick* on the film projector and killed that man. It wasn't me and that's all you need to know."

Just as Penny paused for a breath, a woman's voiced boomed through the activity center, *"Jesus Fucking Christ!"* Everyone turned to see Dee Dee Wellborn standing at the entrance escorted by an out of uniform Sergeant Irv Patterson. "What in the hell is going on?"

"The reporter's been hijacked," Reno Parris volunteered. "And Penny's getting some quality air time."

"If it isn't Dee Dee Wellfed," Penny smiled for the first time. "Sit down sister and shut up. In case you haven't noticed, this isn't your show any more."

Dee Dee recognized the seriousness of the situation and followed instructions."

"Now, let me speak before there's another distraction," Penny said. "And move your camera closer," she said to the cameraman.

Skip adjusted his manual focus..

"I want everyone in this room and in this town to know why I wasn't nominated for homecoming queen. In case you're keeping score, the homecoming queen thing happened pre-curse. You could say it was a precursor." Penny's body shook from her own laughter. "Miss Roberts would be so proud of my vocabulary." It was then that she heard a female voice groan in protest. "That had better not be you Linda Dalby or I'll let everyone know what a slut you were for doing college guys instead of our senior guys. Oh, forget her. I don't want to acknowledge her during my fifteen minutes." Penny paused to inhale. "The reason I didn't get nominated for homecoming queen is right there," she said, pointing the microphone at Reno." Every head except Lance's turned in his direction. "Reno Parris ruined by life. I had such high expectations. My mother had been a homecoming queen and she groomed me from the age of four to follow in her footsteps. She put me in ballet when I was six and sent me to modeling classes the minute I became a teenager. I was so embarrassed that I didn't get nominated, I couldn't look her in the face for weeks," Penny's voice cracked. "Reno's such a bastard. He wanted desperately to fuck me one night at the Goleta drive-in but I wouldn't let him because he didn't have a rubber. So what did he do to get even: the cruelest thing imaginable, that's what? He pressured every guy in the senior class not to nominate me. He threatened to kick their asses if they did. And it worked," Penny started to cry. "I didn't get a single vote and –"

When the studio camera came up hot on KEYT anchor Rita Arenas, she was still checking her make-up with a pocket mirror. When she recognized it was her face on the desktop monitor she flinched. "We're back in our Channel Three studios," she said. "Indeed we are." Rita paused briefly. The blank look on her face suggested she was receiving information through her earpiece. "I'm being told," she started again, "we'll return to our live coverage of *Assault at the Sea Breeze: A Reporter Held Hostage*, after a short commercial interruption."

CHAPTER 36

They never said it publicly but both of Edna Pendleton Wright's daughters claimed her death at the age of 100 was the result of her learning of the planned San Marcos class of '62 reunion. Edna, who years ago dropped the Garland from her name after the judge dropped dead from a massive heart attack while banging a young female employee at a swank beachfront hotel, died two days after seeing Dee Dee Wellborn announce the reunion on her own TV station's news. Edna had appeared to her doctors to have finally been gaining ground in her month long bout with pneumonia. Then, boom, she was gone.

"The moment she heard about a reunion," Emily Hurd told family and friends, "she lost her will. For fifty years she'd considered it her civic duty to discipline the class of '62 for their evil deed. I guess she felt the reunion was a sign that the class of '62 was finally mounting an offensive. She knew she didn't have the strength to fight it."

In what became her final official act as President of KEYT, Edna taped a message to staff employees. The video was shot on her patio deck, which overlooked the entire city of Santa Barbara. Edna, who was slightly hunched, appeared frail, her quivering voice reminiscent of an aging Katherine Hepburn.

"I want the following changes implemented immediately," she said, reading slowly from a list she'd prepared. The changes clearly reflected the bitterness that had consumed her last days.

"Remove the suggestion box from the break room. The workers don't run this station. Convert the break room into a workout facility. Some of you are getting too soft for your own good. Increase local sales by ten percent or else. Our salesmen need to cut out the three martini lunches. Begin grooming Lance Vance for a solo anchor position. He is our future." That was the end of her message, which begged for something positive.

Edna's promotion of Lance stunned members of the news department. None of them saw it coming.

"He may be a bulldog in the field," one associate producer was quoted in the News Press, "but he's a pussycat in the anchor's chair. He has the charisma of a wooden Indian."

The day of the announcement staffers began referring to the future anchor as "Lance Advance." Of course, they did it behind his back.

Lance never got the chance to thank Edna; she died while he was practicing anchoring in a small studio adjacent to the one that housed the news set.

CHAPTER 37

As compelling as Lance Vance's being held hostage was to her patrons -- they were now lined up two deep in front of the bar television -- Cha Cha Miranda was not up to watching it to a conclusion. The same could not be said for a pair of hard drinking Coast Guard officers who'd come from the golf course too many hours ago. They were scrambling to put together a ten-dollar per person pool on how long Penny Sexton could hold out.

Not long after she'd clicked on the bizarre TV standoff, after expecting to see the news, Cha Cha realized the time was at hand for her to finally come forward. She'd been waiting for a push for fifty guilt-ridden years. God bless Penny Sexton. Cha Cha promised herself she'd visit Penny in jail once this was over. If only she could remember her from their days as cheerleading rivals.

Cha Cha was surprised by the internal calm her decision had produced. Ten minutes ago she was angry and her muscles were under lockdown from an argument with her new chef over how much chicken should go into a chicken

Chili Colorado. Alfonso, the chef, was inclined toward excess. "Why don't you throw in the fucking chicken's feet too," Cha Cha had ragged him.

Amid cries from a drunken couple at a back table to turn up the volume on the TV, Cha Cha began putting her plan in motion. "Take over for me," she instructed Vicky, one of her longtime waitresses. "There's something I must do. You'll have to close tonight. Make sure the tables are set for tomorrow. I know you'll take good care of my baby."

Having officially entrusted Casa de Cha Cha to someone other than herself for one of the few times in thirty-eight years, Cha Cha purposefully walked the length of the bar and slipped into her small office adjacent to the men's restroom. Once the door closed, she leaned back against it and took a deep, soothing breath. It seemed to energize her. After checking to make sure her office door was locked, she thumbed through a progression of numbers that was as familiar to her as her own phone number and opened a padlock on the door to a small storage room that was located behind her tiny desk. Immediately, she began sifting through stacks of boxes -- mostly business receipts -- that she'd kept there for years. She knew exactly what she was looking for: a single piece of evidence that would shine a floodlight on the mystery surrounding the evening of June 19th 1962. She was looking for a Virgin Valley Pictures business card. She knew she still had it, but she worried Penny's standoff would end before she could locate it.

CHAPTER 38

Vernon decided the Pepsi truck was a magnet for the cops, so he and Cecil walked a couple blocks east of where it had coughed to a stop and began hitchhiking.

"We're going to freeze to death out here, Vernon."

"Stop complaining, Cecil. "Jeez, we're in California in June, how bad can it be?'

"My joints are in their November, Vernon. How long have I been taking glucosamine for God sakes? The temperature gets below fifty and I stiffen up worse than old sneakers. Why do you think I moved to Arizona, for the buys on the turquoise jewelry?"

"Is that why you move like you're auditioning for a walker?"

Cecil mumbled something that Vernon couldn't hear. "What did you say?"

"Nobody's going to stop for a couple of fossils waddling on the side of the road this late at night."

"We might get lucky, you never know."

"The last time you got lucky you had to pay five-hundred dollars for it, plus another hundred for a room with HBO."

"Yeah, but I didn't jizz all over myself."

Just then a late model Jeep Grand Cherokee approached them. The driver flashed its brights before slowing and pulling over to the curb. Certain they'd managed a ride, Vernon and Cecil scampered toward the Jeep. The front passenger window was open when they finally pulled alongside.

"Where you boys headed?" the driver said.

"L.A.," Cecil said, wheezing from his short run.

"This time of night?"

"We hadn't planned it that way," Cecil said and then coughed heavily.

"Wow," Vernon said, finally getting a decent look at the driver. "We weren't expecting a gorgeous redhead to stop for us."

"We figured it would be some redneck drunk with an attitude." Cecil added.

"Sounds like the ex-boyfriend I just kicked the shit out of back at that Sea Something motel."

"Sea Breeze?" Artie said, his brain suddenly spinning.

"That's the one. Hop in, fellas. My name's Pearl."

Vernon didn't respond right away.

Cecil was too busy massaging his knees to take up the slack in the conversation.

Pearl, who, after her blowup with Reno had decided to visit friends in Riverside, put the Jeep in gear and sped off in the direction of the freeway. She drove several miles without either of her passengers speaking. "Cat got your tongues, fellas?"

"No. No. Sorry," Vernon said. "I was just thinking."

"They had better not be dirty thoughts."

"We're gentlemen hitchhikers."

"No such thing as a gentleman anything."

"You seem rather angry toward men," Cecil said.

"The only thing men are truly good for," Pearl said with a grin, "is getting the toilet seat wet every damned time."

"Have you ever considered anger -- "

Vernon elbowed Cecil's ribs. It was a clear signal for him to shut up. "So you're familiar with the Sea Breeze, are you Pearl?"

"I just stopped off there no more than forty-five minutes ago. I was spying on my boyfriend who was getting too friendly with an old flame from high school."

"Well, maybe you could do us a favor," Vernon said, ignoring Pearl's misfortune.

"I thought I was?"

"Instead of hauling us all the way to L.A. and having to listen to Cecil here complain about not being able to find a joint lubricant that works, I'm wondering if you would consider taking us back to the Sea Breeze?"

Pearl shot a cross-eyed look at Vernon.

"Or better yet, how would you feel about picking up our van from the Sea Breeze parking lot and driving it to a mutually agreed upon location?"

Pearl grinned. "You guys in some kind of trouble?"

"Let's just say we're off the motel manager's mailing list," Vernon said.

A block before the entrance to the freeway Pearl suddenly steered the Jeep into an empty Burger King parking lot and brought it to a stop. "How much you willing to pay for the favor?" she said.

"Fifteen *Power Stroke* drivers," Vernon said. "We use the van to transport them.'

"From where they belong to where they don't, I'm guessing."

"They'd bring about three-thousand dollars." Vernon said."

"Black market?"

"Of course."

"My luck, it'll probably get me in jail," Pearl laughed. "Tell you what, I've been running a little short on adventure lately; I'll do it for twenty of those drivers."

Vernon and Cecil handed over the keys to the van to Pearl and she offered them her Jeep. They agreed to meet and swap vehicles at an all night truck stop at the outskirts of town.

CHAPTER 39

Zeke Clayton was mad at himself for letting Enrique Zendejas drive his Mercedes for him. "Step on it, Enrique," he said. "Christ they'll have their second reunion before we get there."

"Don't want to wreck your new car, boss."

"I'll get another one."

"Yes, you would."

Zeke periodically checked the time on his watch. Enrique punched the Mercedes a little bit more each time he did. "You gonna give your boy a whipping boss?"

Zeke shook his head no. "Don' have to with this stuff," he said, pulling a zip-lock bag of gank from his jacket pocket.

"Is that some of your good shit?"

"Are you kidding? The primo Columbian marching powder is just for me and my ladies."

"That's not enough toot to buy off your son, Zeke. You need a Hefty bag for Scott."

"It's not for his consumption. You're going to plant it on him and the cops are going to find it. I've got friends in high places, here."

"You worked the chief, didn't you?"

"Lonnie does the trick every time."

At the mention of Lonnie a police unit on code three screamed past the Mercedes. It was headed in the direction of the Sea Breeze, which, if Zeke's memory served him right, was only a couple blocks ahead. "Shit! They're going to beat us there, Enrique."

"I work better when there's chaos, boss."

"I like your optimism, Enrique."

Enrique said nothing in response. He took a deep breath and stomped on the gas pedal. The tires on the Mercedes screeched like angry zoo monkeys. Within seconds they were on the tail of the police unit.

"Now you turn into Speed Racer," Zeke said with a grin.

"Shit!" Enrique said, laying heavy on the brakes, "you see what I see?"

"Cops everywhere."

"They've got the whole intersection blocked off. And look, crime scene tape at the entrance to the parking lot. Jesus, this is some serious shit going down."

"There's a sniper....no, two snipers -- SWAT guys -- on the roof," Zeke said. "After shooing *Midnight Seige*, I can spot a sniper with my eyes closed." Zeke reached across and grabbed Enrique's shoulder. "Light's, camera, action. They're playing out my script before I've finished putting it on paper. Hot damn! This is selling tickets to a movie that hasn't been made."

Zeke popped his seat belt and started to open his door. Enrique's firm grip of his bicep stopped him.

"You sure you want to play hardball with Scott? You've always backed off in the past."

"Taking my money is one thing, taking liberties with my creation is another."

"I see where you're coming from, boss."

"I don't think you do, Enrique."

Inside the activity center the standoff continued despite two more commercial interruptions and a suggestion by Penny that Whitney Crawford open new nominations for homecoming queen.

"Not until I finish cross examining you," Whitney said. "You're not off the hook yet."

Lance Vance continued to show remarkable poise under scissors. Bleeding steadily, although not profusely, he continued to facilitate Penny's ranting and at one point even solicited group feedback, which turned his cameraman Skip into a human pretzel as he tried to point his lens at people in front and in back of him. Penny, however, quickly put that idea to bed, saying, "This is my show, we do what I say, not you, cutie."

Lance gingerly nodded that he understood.

Once she'd heard the police sirens advancing on the Sea Breeze, Penny made it clear via the live coverage that police were to take her instructions from what they heard on TV. She was emphatic about not wanting to negotiate face-to-face. "I see a copper in this building and cutie here will be able to breathe through his neck," Penny said.

She was unaware of Sergeant Patterson who, after assessing the situation, had left Dee Dee Wellborn's side and quietly slipped to the back of the room, mixing with some of the guests a good distance from where Penny and Lance were occupying center stage. He held his position for a few minutes, waiting for the right time to make a move. He recognized there was an opportunity to be a hero in front of a live television audience. That, he reasoned, could catapult him to the vacant captain's position before sunrise.

"You fixin' to do something about this mess?" Edgar Peoples said to Sergeant Patterson as he moved alongside the big man in the quietest section of the activity center.

The sergeant eyeballed Edgar's leather with his best Joe Friday look. "What makes you say that?" the sergeant growled.

"You keep tapping your piece under your sport jacket."

"Little nosey, aren't you?"

"I've seen enough TV shoot-em-ups to be able to spot an off-duty cop half-a-block away."

"Good for you, boy. Was TV your major?"

"Boy? That's a fresh concept."

"Shut the fuck up, nigger."

"There's another one. Next you're going to tell me *Amos 'n Andy* was you're favorite TV show."

Without responding, the sergeant suddenly tucked his chin to his chest, pumped his arms piston-like and bolted in Penny's direction, knocking partygoers aside with each stride. "You're ass is mine," he hollered as he rushed to within a couple feet of her and launched his body like a missile.

Somehow, considering the amount she'd had to drink, Penny's peripheral vision was still acute enough for her to react to Sergeant Patterson's approach. Instinctively, she called on her latent athletic skills and without moving the scissors from Lance's jugular, she executed a subtle drop-step followed by a nifty side-slip that any NBA center would be proud to have in his repertoire. Penny's evasive action resulted in Patterson's grabbing nothing but air as he flew past her, his momentum carrying him head-first into the only support beam in the entire activity center. It caused such a loud thud that the coke machine miraculously kicked on, spewing dust everywhere. The sergeant lay motionless at the base of the beam, blood oozing from a nasty gash over his left eyebrow. Ever alert, Skip had captured every step of his courageous attempt to end the stand-off. Like any heads up news executive, Channel Three's special coverage producer called for one replay after another of the event, no doubt severely damaging any hope Sergeant Patterson might have had for a promotion.

"Jesus fucking Christ! Somebody call for help!" Dee Dee yelled, as she rushed to the sergeant's side. Without hesitation she ripped her bra out from under her gold silk blouse and placed it under his head for comfort.

"It's a fucking D-cup if anyone's wondering."

"Watch your language, Dee Dee Wellfed," Penny said, raising her voice. "This is family TV."

"Not now. Not after you've traumatized every kid under thirteen with this senseless blood letting."

"Oh stop with your bitching, Dee Dee. It's not enough blood to test for iron deficiency. Besides, everyone knows life before thirteen has no inherent meaning or value. It's playtime. It's when your best friends are imaginary, your best dress is imitation Barbi and you think you're better than boys at everything."

"When did you open up a practice, Penny?"

"When I realized that your stone cold cop over there on the floor is the second guy you've been with tonight."

Dee Dee responded by rattling off a wagonload of obscenities at Penny. The Channel Three producer wisely viewed Dee Dee's tirade as an opportunity for yet another commercial interruption and instructed Lance to toss it back to the studio anchors.

CHAPTER 40

Rita Arenas and her co-anchor Tyler Tew had been facilitating Penny Sexton's hostage drama for almost an hour, re-setting the scene on numerous occasions and tossing repeatedly to Lance Vance. Both Rita and Tyler had stumbled over words in recent minutes, a sure sign of anchor fatigue. Neither had ever worked beyond the regularly scheduled news signoff at 11:30 PM.

Coming out of a commercial break, Rita was caught speaking to someone out of camera range. "Tell me Lance isn't milking this for his career. We damn well better get overtime for his little folly," she said. Realizing she'd been caught again, Rita took a deep breath before beginning. "Sorry if you happened to catch some of our shop talk," she said, her face as red as her lipstick. "Anyway, welcome back to our continuing live coverage of *Assault at the Sea Breeze: A Reporter Held Hostage*," she said, her face locked in the same stern "I'm doing my best to appear deeply concerned" expression that all anchors must minor in as career pre-requisites. Rita's droopy eyebrows signaled her waning spark.

Then, as if a voice decreed she "get perky," Rita morphed into Katie Couric, with an assist from the TelePromter. "Everyone at Channel Three News is happy to welcome D& L Motors as title sponsor of our continuing live, local coverage of *Assault at the Sea Breeze: A Reporter Held Hostage.* The good folks at D & L Motors want to remind you that the best deal in a used car is automatic when you shop for your next vehicle at D & L."

Both anchors then appeared in a two shot and Tyler Tew seemed anxious to stick in his two cents. "Hats off to the guys in Channel Three's sales department," he said with a toothy grin. "This hostage situation is barely into its second hour and already they've locked up a title sponsor and they accomplished it on a weekend night. That's got to be some kind of world record."

Rita road the same wave. "Just goes to show you that KEYT has talent that extends beyond the newsroom, Tyler. Makes you proud to work here."

The director then cut to a single shot of Tyler, whose face immediately changed from happy to sad. "Speaking of our newsroom, one of our own, Lance Vance has endured a perilous sixty-plus minutes as a hostage…"

CHAPTER 41

Vernon and Cecil were relieved at the sight of their white Aerostar pulling into the Vaquero Truck Stop parking lot. They'd waited on Pearl less than twenty minutes after dropping her off a couple blocks away from the Sea Breeze.

"Suppose she's that efficient in bed?" Cecil wondered out loud as the two watched from the front seat of Pearl's jeep.

"She doesn't look like the efficient type, Cecil. For Chrissakes, you expect a woman with tits like hers to be efficient -- slam bam, thank you, Sam.."

"I get your point, Vernon."

Pearl had a bounce to her step as she approached the Jeep. "Piece of cake," she said. "The police were preoccupied with some Looney Toon chick who's holding a TV reporter hostage. They paid no attention to me."

"Great work, Pearl," Vernon said.

"If it's so great, how come I don't see twenty of those what-do-you-call-em drivers in the back of my jeep?"

"We've learned not to trust anyone," Cecil said.

Pearl placed her hands on her hips. "Well, trust in the fact I will kick your collective asses into next week if I don't see those golf clubs resting in the back of my Jeep in fifteen minutes."

"Gottcha," Vernon said. "There was never any need to think we wouldn't deliver."

"Yeah, and don't worry, I'm on the pill, honey." Pearl said, with a grin as wide as the grille on her 4X4.

With Vernon leading in the van, Pearl followed the two to a storage park on Milpas Street. They were greeted at the gate by a sign that instructed customers wishing to enter after midnight to use the intercom to contact the night manager.

"Shit!" Vernon said. "We've got to clear out our inventory tonight, Cecil. The manager is going to be suspicious of us coming in here in the middle of the night. I don't want him snooping around and finding our clubs."

"With our luck he probably wouldn't be a golfer and we'd have no leverage, Vernon."

"Good thinking, Cecil."

"My God, an actual compliment. You're softening in your old age, Vernon."

After they'd loaded Pearl's Jeep with the promised twenty *Power Strokes* and said good-bye to her, Vernon and Cecil decided to head for L.A. after all. Cecil was pretty sure he could drum up a buyer there. He just hoped his Santa Barbara contact would understand it was too risky for them to remain there another minute. It wasn't good for business to stiff a customer, especially when he's a crook, too. "We dodged a few bullets tonight," Cecil said, as much for his own ears as Vernon's. They had just passed the city limits sign heading south on 101. The lights of Montecito were just coming into view.

"Let's save the confetti for another time," Vernon said. "Every time we think we're out of the woods with this damn heist, shit happens."

"What else could possibly go wrong, Vernon?"

The words had barely left Cecil's mouth when the Aerostar's steering wheel locked on Vernon.

"Power steering's gone!" Vernon shouted. The Aerostar veered across two lanes and a gravel shoulder and was boring in on an ice plant-covered ditch.

"Hit the brakes," Cecil hollered.

Instead of the brakes, Vernon, in his haste, slammed his foot hard on the accelerator.

"Shit!" Vernon said.

"Fuck!" Cecil said.

The Aerostar slammed into the ditch, kicking up a storm of dirt and ice plant. The impact caused the hood to pop open. By the time Vernon and Cecil were able to free themselves from the wreckage and check for damage, the radiator had begun spewing steam like it was an active volcano.

"Were fucked," Vernon said, hands on hips and shaking his head.

"Remarkable perception," Cecil said.

For once Vernon ignored Cecil's cynicism. "Let's get moving. We've got the railroad tracks for cover. There's enough of an embankment to keep us hidden from freeway passersby."

"So now we're walking to L.A?" Cecil said. "I can't even make eighteen holes in a cart any more."

"Jeez, Cecil. Have a brain. We'll grab all the clubs we can hand carry. We'll break into the first unoccupied place we come to. We'll stash the clubs and then come back for more."

"This is going to kill my joints, Vernon."

"Better that than having the cops find a van full of drivers and throw us in the joint."

Within ten minutes after they'd left the van with the first load of *Power Strokes* tucked under their arms, Vernon and Cecil came upon an isolated bungalow located on the frontage road to the freeway not far from the Miramar Hotel. It was well shielded by a large oak tree and oleander bushes. A dozen or more newspapers strewn across the driveway told Vernon that no one had been there in some time.

With Cecil's endorsement, Vernon picked the lock and they entered. The small unit was richly furnished in Italian leather and immaculately kept: albeit missing anything that would remotely be considered an accessory. There were no signs that anyone had been there recently. However, there was no way either could explain the bed sheets being turned down.

"Think anyone's planning on using this?" Cecil asked, staring at the bed.

"I am," Vernon said. "Once we get the rest of the *Power Strokes*."

"Count me out, Vernon. I've made my last haul."

"What do you mean?"

"My arthritis is killing me -- neck, back, knees."

"You are worthless, you know."

"But I'm customer service and you can't deal without me, can you?"

"Fuck me naked," Vernon said as he headed out the front door. "If anyone is looking for me tell them I'm out collecting wood -- fairway wood."

CHAPTER 42

Flanked by Enrique Zendejas, Zeke Clayton walked briskly toward the police command post that consisted of a large portable table, four director's chairs, a TV monitor and a coffee maker. It was positioned in the middle of the Sea Breeze parking lot.

"Whose in charge?" Zeke said, his nonchalance making it appear as if his arrival was the more important of the events currently taking place.

"Who wants to know?" a short, round, fair-skinned officer replied from his seat in front of the TV. He was holding a cell phone to his ear.

"Zeke Clayton."

"And you are?"

"Surely..."

"Surely, I don't give a – "

"Compliments of the Chief," Zeke said as he handed over his.business card, which prominently displayed the Chief's signature and some other writing.

The officer studied the card carefully, then smiled for the first time and said, "I'm Captain Crenshaw. I enjoy your movies." He shook Zeke's hand.

Captain Crenshaw, who'd finished a bitter "also ran" to Junior in the selection process for chief, was suddenly distracted by a response on his cell. "Is this Penny Sexton I'm speaking with?"

Zeke could hear a female voice coming from the earpiece.

"Damn, I can't get her to talk to me," the captain said to no one in particular. "All she wants to do is talk on TV." The captain turned back to Zeke. "Sorry for the interruption."

"No problem."

"I do have to ask why you want to go inside. It's an unsafe situation and one that could possibly get worse once the LA stations park their satellite trucks here and try to bully for the best camera positions inside the center."

"I just want to visit my son. He's attending the party. Haven't seen him in years. Saw his mug in the background on a promotion for the eleven o'clock news."

"As long as it doesn't freak our gal with the scissors. If it does, I'll personally come and get you."

Zeke took a couple of steps in the direction of the entrance to the activity center and then stopped and turned back toward Captain Crenshaw. "I figured the chief would be all over this scene."

"We're having a problem locating him."

"That's unfortunate," Zeke said, offering a slight smile.

Judging by Captain Crenshaw's puzzled look, Zeke guessed the good Captain had no idea what to make of his last remark.

Several hours into the hostage drama, cell phone activity among partygoers reached a crescendo. It sounded like a shopping mall the day before Christmas. Friends and relatives watching on TV were checking on the welfare of class members. Holly Murchison was one of many who'd received a call. She was standing next to Reno when it came in. She listened for a minute or so and finally said, "You're probably right." She hung up shortly after.

"It was Shannon, wasn't it?" Reno said.

"Yes."

"Shit!" Reno said. "He wants you out of here, right?"

"Immediately. I've never heard him demand anything before."

"Did you tell him you were in good hands?"

"I don't think that's something he'd care to hear."

Reno placed his hand on Holly's arm and peered into her eyes. "You're comfortable with him, aren't you?"

"I am. It's just that – "

"Go. It's where you belong. Besides, if you did let me get into your pants tonight, you'd spend the rest of your life regretting it."

"No," Holly said with a warm smile. "I'd probably kick myself for not allowing it to happen back when."

"That's the nicest thing anyone's said to me in months."

"You're a good guy, Reno, even though you've spent a lifetime trying to prove you're not. I feel privileged to know the truth."

"Jeez," Reno said, nervously shifting his weight from one leg to the other. "This is way too heavy for me."

As he was searched his mind for his parting words, Reno heard Penny holler for him. Several others picked it up and began chanting his name. He didn't have a clue what she wanted, but Reno was a sucker for any kind of an audience.

"Gotta go, girl. Give my best to Shannon, the lucky bastard."

"Be careful with Penny," Holly said, planting a friendly kiss on Reno's cheek. "And ditch the Tanya Harding wannabe. You can do better than her."

Reno wouldn't permit the lump in his throat to fully form. In defense, he turned away from Holly and hustled over to where Penny was holding Lance Vance hostage. He parked himself directly in front of her. It was as close as he'd been to her all night. As Penny presented him the microphone, Reno couldn't help noticing how frazzled she looked. She was perspiring at the temples and above her lip; her makeup was converging on her cheeks and it was clearly an effort for her to hold the scissors to Lance's jugular. Reno was puzzled by Lance's unwillingness to try and escape. It seemed to him the opportunity was ever present and the task not all that difficult.

"This is the aforementioned Reno Parris," Penny said, looking directly at Lance Vance. "Lance, this is Reno." Lance Vance shifted his eyes as far as he could to his right to try and get a better look.

The instant the introductions were complete, Penny's cell phone rang. It was an effort for her to answer the phone and hold the scissors on Lance. "Why do you keep calling, Captain Kangaroo?" Penny said. "I told you three times already. I'm not ending this until I've had my say." She paused to listen. "It could take another five minutes or five hours. Now don't call me again. Just watch TV and listen, if that's not asking you to display too many communication skills at once."

Lance Vance felt a need to inform the viewer. "That was Captain Edwin Crenshaw of the Santa Barbara Police Department. He is the department's chief hostage negotiator. He's credited with the recent surrender of a man who held six people hostage at the Bank of Montecito in – "

"Okay, okay," Penny said. "This isn't about Captain Kangaroo. It's about me. Now lets get on with it. Reno," she said, motioning him even closer. "I want you to take the microphone." She handed it to him. "Think of this as my payback."

Reno acknowledged the comment with a nod of his head.

"I want you to conduct a viewers poll. We're going interactive here, tonight folks."

"What do you want me to ask?" Reno said, his wrinkled brow reflecting the bizarre twist the hostage drama seemed to be taking.

"Ask them if they think I should have been nominated for homecoming queen. Tell them to call the station with a yes or a no."

Reno turned to face the camera. "There it is ladies and gentleman. Your chance to turn back the clock." Reno turned to look at Lance. "What number do they call, Lance?"

"553-5350," Lance said.

"How about we try to accomplish this in fifteen minutes," Reno said, turning back to the camera. "Should Penny Sexton have been nominated for homecoming queen, yeah or ney? And, while I'm at it I'll accept orders -- Visa or MasterCard -- for the Greatest Hits of the Sixties CD, new from Remembrance Records. Hoping to get lucky tonight? Get motivated by listening to Johnny Mathis sing 'Chances

Are.' Fats Domino will thrill you with 'Blueberry Hill,' and travel back through the memories of your mind with Rick Nelson and 'Travelin' Man'..."

"Well," a red-eyed and slightly said exasperated Rita Arenas said as the production switched back to the studio. "Humor is the last thing you'd expect in a hostage drama. We've had it all tonight and we'll continue with our live coverage of *Assault at the Sea Breeze: An Oportunist Held Hostage*...I mean a reporter held hostage, after this word from our latest contributing sponsor, Jiffy Bail Bonds, who promise 'no others can compete when it comes to getting you back on the street'."

CHAPTER 43

Janet Nyborg, who had returned to live in Santa Barbara after her son left for college, never missed Channel Three's late news. As a result, she was probably one of the best-informed citizens in the community. She felt comfortable discussing everything from waterfront zoning to a solution to Santa Barbara's growing homeless population, and as a result, had become a regular at city council meetings. She frequently voiced her opinion on the issues at public forums and was labeled the "people's watchdog" in a News Press feature story profiling her. Not surprisingly, city administrators considered her a giant pain in the ass.

Ironically, the news wasn't why she watched Channel Three. It was her only chance anymore to see her son, Lance Vance. They'd become estranged three years ago when Lance had insisted she finally tell him who his natural father was. He'd hit a rough patch in his life with a live-in lover -- Andrea someone -- who'd cheated on him. It sparked a six-month period of introspection and reflection. He refused to accept that Janet didn't know the father's identity.

Janet, who was dressed in jeans, a Grateful Dead sweat-shirt and sandals and had just finished washing her long blonde hair, called her neighbors from the next apartment and invited them to watch the hostage drama. She was proud of the courage and poise Lance was exhibiting and she wanted to share it with somebody, not just sit alone in her tiny apartment, which she did more often than she liked to admit.

The Walkers, Bob and Edith, had never met Lance, but they knew all about him from Janet. They knew enough about his drinking problem to wonder aloud if he must be going through withdrawal while he was on the air at this late hour.

"His adrenalin is compensating for it," Janet suggested. She offered the Walkers, both in their seventies and mar-ried to a healthy lifestyle, some chocolate almond-rocca ice cream, but they passed.

The Walkers, who'd moved to Santa Barbara from Champaign, Illinois in just the last year, inquired about the story behind the story they were watching and Janet obliged, detailing the saga of the curse on the class of '62.

Janet also explained to the Walkers that she should have graduated with San Marcos' class of '62 and included the reason why she didn't. But after she finished that, she fell strangely silent, acting as if the Walker's were no longer present. The Walkers tried to make conversation, but Janet wouldn't respond, choosing instead to stare at the TV as if she'd suddenly come under a mysterious spell. Finally, Bob and Edith put their heads together when Janet got up to go to the bathroom and agreed that Janet must be undergoing some kind of psychological trauma, watching her son in a perilous situation and all. They decided it was best to leave her to her thoughts, whatever they might be.

As soon as the Walkers left her apartment -- Bob did decide on some almond-roca to go -- Janet turned off all the lights except the one over the stove, and called for a cab. "I want you to take me to the Sea Breeze motel, she said. "I'm in a hurry." She retrieved an old raincoat from her closet, placed it over her shoulders and continued to watch TV until the taxi driver knocked on her front door some twenty minutes later.

CHAPTER 44

Zeke Clayton entered the Sea Breeze's activity center just as Penny Sexton was receiving – via Lance Vance – Channel Three's first returns on the question whether she should have been nominated for homecoming queen.

"It's running three-to-one," Lance said, taking a deep swallow as if his throat was hurting him. He sounded a little hoarse as well.

"For me?" Penny said excitedly

"Yes."

"How many callers?"

"Hundred and forty, so far."Penny raised her hand, the one that wasn't holding the scissors, and made a fist. "Keep the yes votes coming, Santa Barbara," she said, smiling for the first time in several hours.

After a second appeal for votes Penny finally noticed Zeke Clayton making his way through the activity center, stopping every few feet to sign autographs. Penny's eyes got big and suddenly looked less weary as she witnessed Zeke throw his arms around Edgar Peoples and give him a lengthy bear hug. They had moved to within a few feet of her without Zeke acknowledging her. She heard them exchange greetings but didn't have a clue what Zeke meant when he said to Edgar, "I see by your threads you're still getting my checks." Before they separated Penny, heard Zeke thank him for taking care of the Janet thing.

"Just protecting my ass," she heard Zeke say.

Penny took a second to quietly chastise herself for having too much to drink to make sense of their conversation.

Even though he seldom visits Santa Barbara, Zeke's celebrity insures him a high profile in the town where he grew up. "You, you," Penny muttered, pointing the microphone at Zeke. "You're Zeke Clayton, aren't you?"

Zeke, who'd moved from his encounter with Edgar and was signing a piece of sheet music put forth by one of *The Occasions,* acknowledged Penny with a slight nod of his head.

"I loved Adrienne Waters in *Color Me Your Sister*. I could so identify with her trials and tribulations," Penny gushed.

Lance Vance quietly interrupted Penny to inform her that it was time for another commercial break, but Penny wasn't about to let an opportunity to have Zeke Clayton participate in her drama slip by.

"Come join us," Penny said to Zeke. "It's not every day that a big star drops in on your life."

Without hesitation, Zeke moved closer, finally reaching Penny's side after several ex-tenth grade classmates tried to corral him with offers of free drinks.

"Welcome to my – "

"Your show," Zeke said, flashing the brilliant smile that had adorned so many entertainment magazines over the years.

"Yeah, my show," Penny said, the twinkle in her eyes fully restored. "I like that." She turned momentarily in Lance's direction. "Have your people refer to this as the *Penny Sexton Show* from now on, Lance."

Lance's, make-up was beginning to smudge from perspiration. "I don't have to tell them anything. They hear everything you say."

"That's right. I keep forgetting. TV is so new to me."

For the first time since he'd entered the activity center, Zeke spotted Scott through the maze of people's heads. He was standing near the bar helping Linda Dalby with her coat. They appeared to be leaving, which prompted Zeke to move quickly from Penny's side.

"Where are you going? Can I be in one of your movies?" Penny shouted like a child begging for a birthday pony ride.

"Gotta take care of something," Zeke said without looking back at Penny. He aggressively made his way through the partygoers. "Scott. Wait!" he hollered as he caught a glimpse of Linda Dalby disappearing through the side exit.

Scott, who was not yet through the door, stopped and turned toward Zeke; his eyes appeared glazed, the muscles in his face appeared taut.

"If only he'd have used that look in my movies" Zeke said to himself while acknowledging that it was a strange thought given the moment. "Christ, don't run off. I made a special trip here to say hello. I saw you on TV."

"My date isn't feeling well," Scott said.

"Linda, please come back and join us," Zeke said, hoping she could hear through the tiny crack in the door. She stepped back into the activity center only seconds later.

"Long time, no!" Linda's tone reeked of cynicism.

"Indeed, it has been awhile," Zeke smiled, extending his hand to Linda. "You look fabulous."

She reciprocated with a hand but not a smile then glanced at Scott as if she were looking for direction from him. Just then Enrique Zendejas made it a foursome.

"You're looking much better than the last time I saw you, son."

"Since I was feeling like death warmed over the last time I saw you, I can't accept that as a compliment."

"Off the drugs, son?"

"Thanks to Linda's help."

"How did this unusual coupling take place?"

Linda laughed softly. "It's a conspiracy, Zeke." She smiled and then shook her head.

"We haven't got time for even the short version," Scott said.

I've got all night."

"Well, we don't." Scott placed his arm around Linda's shoulders and pivoted her in the direction of the door. "It's been swell, Dad."

"Doubly for me," Linda said.

"Before you go, I want to know what you're doing here, Scott."

"And then you're going to tell me to be in by two."

"Don't get smart with me, Scott. I'm still your father."

"You're wrong. All you ever were was a sperm donor."

Zeke paused to take off his overcoat. "Before you leave you are gong to explain your presence here."

"Everybody has to be some place."

"You're fucking trying to steal my idea for a movie about this aren't you?" The veins in Zeke's neck suddenly became the size of railroad tracks. "Admit it."

"Wow!" Scott said, breaking into a smile for the first time. "Paranoia rules."

"Just protecting my property, son."

"Why are you so obsessed with this story to begin with?"

"Lets just say I have a vested interest in it," Zeke said, squaring his feet for better balance should junior decided to get physical.

Scott shook his head. "Your probably the guy who did the skin flick thing. These people are likely barking up the wrong tree."

Zeke's face quickly turned red. Without another word he thrust his coat into Scott's chest. Scott let it fall to the floor.

"As a matter of fact, Dad, Linda has agreed to help me write both a book and a screenplay about that night," he lied. "We're here collecting anecdotes from her former classmates. In return I've promised her the part of Edna Pendleton Wright. How does that grab you?"

Zeke knew from experience that if he took a step toward Scott he'd get him to make the first move. Scott bit on the tactic, ripping off his coat, flipping it on a chair and chest bumping Zeke. "You want some of me, old man?"

Out of the corner of his eye Zeke could see Enrique retrieve Scott's overcoat and reach into a pocket. "The only thing I want is for you to get a new last name."

Scott's eyes rolled back in his head an instant before he lunged at his father with a looping right hand that caught nothing but air.

Zeke held Scott off with a straight arm to his chest. "That's why you didn't cut it in the movies, son. You swing like a girl."

Scott threw another lame right that bounced harmlessly off his father's shoulder. Zeke responded by ramming his face into Scott's chest, wrapping his arms around him and driving through him like he was a tackling dummy. Scott landed hard on his back and gasped for air as Zeke landed squarely on his chest. For nearly a minute they grappled on the floor without either getting the advantage.

On cue, Enrique beat a path to where Captain Crenshaw was camped in the parking lot with word of the altercation. Five officers were dispatched to the side entrance of the activity center. The officers quickly separated the combatants without Penny ever becoming aware of the fracas. Just as quickly they confiscated Scott's overcoat. One of the officers said, "Bingo," as he produced a Ziploc bag containing white powder."

"Want to tell me what's in here?" a hairy-armed sergeant said to Scott.

"I don't want to tell you shit," Scott said, his eyeballs red with rage. "Ask him." Scott pointed at Zeke. "He's the one who put it there." Scott spit in the direction of his dad but missed.

Before anyone could say another word, Scott was whisked out of the activity center and into an awaiting squad car.

Linda stayed behind briefly to address Zeke. "My guess is you won't be nominated for this year's parenting Oscar." She turned and walked out of the building.

Zeke followed her into the parking lot but stopped to watch the squad car carrying Scott disappear into the night. "Nice work," he said to Enrique.

Enrique shook his head. "There must have been more information on that honorary captain's card than your name and address."

"I don't hand over Lonnie without a good compensation package, Enrique."

"The undisputed heavyweight champion of influence pedaling. That's you, boss."

"Sometimes I amaze myself," Zeke said. He motioned with a jerk of his head for Enrique to follow him back into the activity center.

"You sure you want to go back in there? You got what you came for."

"I'm sure. There is a script being written for me in there. I don't have to pay for a writer this way."

"Makes business sense."

"I majored in business sense, Enrique."

CHAPTER 45

Had she not realized, once she'd reached her car in the parking lot, that she'd forgotten her cell phone back in the office, Cha Cha Miranda would not have known she was about to cross paths with Zeke Clayton for the first time since that matinee at the Granada Theatre. At once she was energized by seeing him on her TV screen with Penny, and apprehensive. Her concern was that if she didn't have the goods to bring him down -- she was confident she did -- he'd surely retaliate as he did so long ago when she witnessed him take a shotgun to all four tires on her dad's pickup truck. Even today, Cha Cha got goose bumps at the recall of her dad having to work overtime every day for a month to pay for new tires.

It was the television image of a boozed-up, tired and confused Penny Sexton that occupied Cha Cha's mind as she maneuvered her Toyota 4-Runner through a series of stoplights on lower State Street. How the landscape of Santa Barbara's main street had changed in recent years, she noted. Gone were the old name department stores, drug stores and banks; replaced by a thousand specialty boutiques, coffee houses and restaurants. Cha Cha found it depressing to one day discover that where she once could inspect the new line of washers and dryers along with the latest TV models, she could now purchase a decorative face mask with a design representing practically every culture in the world -- for just under a hundred dollars.

At the stop light a block from the Sea Breeze, Cha Cha filled the wait by again inspecting her purse for the all important business card that along with her testimony was sure to rock the reunion and shock those watching Penny's hostage standoff on TV.

She could tell the card was still there by the feel of its crisp edges. In the silence of her heart she again scolded herself for waiting so long.

CHAPTER 46

Fully clothed and exhausted from six trips to the van and back for the *Power Strokes*, Vernon collapsed face down on the bungalow's king size bed. He was too tired to even consider taking off his clothes.

Just as he was teetering on the brink sleep, Cecil came into the bedroom with a shopping bag full of complaints that he felt compelled to voice. "There are no towels for a shower, no plates or cups, no toilet paper, no nothing. All we've got is a couch, a love seat and the bed you're soiling with your dirty clothes," Cecil said. "And I'm hungry as hell and there's nothing to eat."

"It's a good thing you weren't born in frontier days," Vernon said, trying to wipe the drowsiness from his eyes. "I can picture you resting your weary head on your saddle wearing the same clothes you've had on for a month. You're parked in front of a camp fire after a fourteenth straight meal of chili beans all the while complaining about the stars being too bright for you to get a decent night's sleep."

"What's your point?"

"I don't know, I was just —"

"What was that?" Cecil whispered.

Voices could be heard at the front of the bungalow.

"Sounds like someone is trying to unlock the door."

"Shit!" Cecil said. "How can deja vu happen all over?"

"The closet," Vernon said, pointing to the huge walk-in closet where he'd stored the *Power Strokes*.

"Here we go again, Vernon."

"This time, keep that pecker of yours under control."

"How do you know it's going to be a couple having sex again?"

"Cause that's how I'm being punished for my evil deeds."

"Watching sex is punishment?"

"You ever hear the expression, 'those who can, do; those who can't, watch'?"

"Never."

"Well, it's the painful truth."

"Shh!" Cecil said. "I think they're inside now."

It wasn't long before Vernon and Cecil determined that it was a man and a woman.

"You're such a beast," they could hear the woman say. "I like a man who can't wait to reach the bedroom."

"I've always wanted to do it on leather," the man said.

"Ooh, ooh, ooh," the woman moaned.

"It's good isn't it, baby?" the man said.

"I don't know yet," the woman whined."

"But..."

"It's your badge. It's scratching the hell out of my boob."

"Sorry."

Cecil elbowed Vernon. "Did she say badge?"

"I think so."

"Shit! We're like Velcro."

"What do you mean?"

"Cops stick to us."

"Where do you come up with shit like that?"

"I was told as far back as grade school I had a creative mind."

"Well, imagine how we're going to get out of this mess."

"With the help of God," Cecil said.

"When did you start playing the God card?"

"At the end of the day God knows we're not crooks. I think he understands we're just enterprising duffers trying to support a golf addiction that's eaten up our nest eggs. It's not like we're dealing drugs, molesting young kids and all. We're just stealing to buy a few more tee times."

"Cecil, you're talking too much. I can't hear the love couple."

"That's cause they're coming in here. Damn!"

Vernon and Cecil could hear the shuffling of feet and the by now unmistakable sound of people shedding their clothes. Vernon said he thought the big clunk he heard was the cop's belt hitting the hardwood floor.

"I hope it was a belt and not his gun," Cecil said.

"We've got to be proactive this time," Vernon whispered.

"What does that mean, Vernon?"

"We have to act, not react. We can't risk them pulling an all nighter and leaving us stuffed in here like last month's laundry."

"My joints are already screaming at me, Vernon."

"Exactly what I mean."

The unidentified man and woman had predictably moved to the bed, which was less than ten feet from the closet where Vernon and Cecil were cloistered.

"It looks like someone's been on this bed," the man said.

"Are you cops always so suspicious?"

"I'm trained to be observant."

"Well come here you big strong man and observe my pussy," the woman said. "See how wet it is for you?"

"Oh, yeah," the man said.

Cecil, who along with Vernon was resting on one knee, switched knees, which required maximum effort. By the time he repositioned himself, Cecil was breathing heavily. "I can't stand it!" he said, his voice rising dangerously close to a normal speaking voice. "Twice in one night? I feel like we're a traveling peep show, for Christ sakes."

After watching his partner's human pretzel act, and certain in his belief that Cecil was going to "go off" again at the sounds of sex, Vernon decided to put his plan into gear. He grabbed the nearest *Power Stroke* and instructed Cecil to do the same. "On the count of three, we go, Cecil. We have to convince the cop we can harm him with the drivers. Then we have to find his gun."

"What if he doesn't have one?"

"Is an accountant ever without a calculator? A lawyer without a billable hours instrument?"

"Suppose not."

"...two, three."

Vernon led the mini-charge from the closet. The door flew open and banged against a doorstop.

"Aah," Vernon groaned as he tried to straighten up.

"Uuh," Cecil moaned as his right knee buckled slightly.

"Ooh," the woman purred as she rode the cop's unit from her position on top.

"Fuck!" the cop shouted as he discovered Vernon and Cecil advancing toward the bed.

As quickly as he could, Vernon closed in on the two as they attempted to untangle. As he reached the side of the bed he slammed the head of his *Power Stroke* against the headboard. Whack! It sounded an awful lot like a gunshot Vernon thought. "Freeze!" Vernon shouted, "and nobody gets hurt."

"Can't you be more original than that?" Cecil said.

"It works on TV."

The cop spoke out. "You'll never get – "

"Shut up!" Vernon said, only then realizing the *Power Stroke* he was pointing at the couple had no head."

"I told you those clubs were crap," Cecil said.

"You shut up too, Cecil."

"Thanks for mentioning my name, Vernon. I have business cards you can pass around later."

The cop placed his hands on the woman's hips and slowly lowered her to one side of him on the bed.

"Where you going, pal?" Vernon said to the cop. Alertly, Vernon tossed his *Power Stroke* on the floor and took the one Cecil was holding. "Get another one," he directed Cecil.

"You really think you can hold me at bay with a golf club?" the cop said.

Without responding Vernon raised his driver over his head and slammed it into a pillow, the club head striking just inches from the cop's head. The whites of the cop's eyes became beacons in the darkness.

"Where's your gun?" Vernon said.

There was no answer so Vernon again slammed his driver against the pillow. It landed even closer to the Chief's head this time.

"I think it's in his shoe," the woman said.

The cop turned to the woman with question marks in both eyes. "Why did –?"

"We have to cooperate. I once worked as a bank teller and that's the first thing they taught us."

"I'd never complain about standing in your line," Cecil said.

"Thank you, Cecil," the woman said.

Cecil quickly searched the cop's shoes and found his revolver. "Got it."

The cop pushed himself into a sitting position, his back against the headboard. "Do you two have any idea who I am?"

"You're a cop."

"I'm not just any cop."

"He's the Chief of Police," the woman said.

"And you're Mrs. Chief," Cecil said with the hint of a hint of laughter creeping into his voice.

"Hah!" the woman said.

"Cheatin' on the old lady, huh Chief? We got us some leverage, Cecil."

"Stop using my name, Vernon."

Vernon ignored his partner. "If you're the chief you must have an unmarked car?"

"Plain old Ford, something," the woman said. "It's parked in the driveway. By the way, you can call me Lonnie."

Vernon brought the head of the *Power Stroke* in front of his face and inspected the logo. "I'll call you princess if you can tell me where the keys are."

"Probably in his pants pocket," Lonnie said.

Vernon found the keys after a quick search and ordered Cecil to make sure they started the Ford in the driveway. While Cecil was gone, Vernon located the chief's handcuffs and had Lonnie tether him to the bed frame. If only he'd had a camera, Vernon thought. He had the chief of police in the ultimate compromising position.

Cecil burst back into the bungalow bedroom with renewed vigor. "Good to go," was his report on the Ford. "And look what I found on the front seat."

"A digital camera?" Vernon said.

"Yep. And some bungy cords in the trunk."

"Perfect," Vernon said, pumping his fist like a twenty-year old.

Cecil bungied Lonnie to the bed frame as well and snapped a picture of the two totally nude lovebirds. Vernon told the chief if any of his men followed them, the love nest pictures would be made public faster than he could say download. "Ever hear of Photobucket, boss?"

Situation in hand, Vernon and Cecil took as many of the remaining *Power Strokes* as the Ford could accommodate and then said their good-byes.

"There are more of the drivers in the closet, chief," Vernon said. "Help yourself."

"They're good for an extra ten yards, chief," Cecil said. "But, the damn things will cause you to spray the ball like...like mace."

The chief raised his head and spoke through gritted teeth. "So you're the ones who are supposed to be making the drop to Artie Santana."

Cecil looked at Vernon. Their faces were studies in disbelief.

"Consider yourself fortunate. We've had him under surveillance for a month."

"Consider us gone," Vernon said. "When we get to our destination I'll radio your 10-20, chief. Stay put until."

"You'll hear from me again," the chief said. "No two old fucks like you will ever one up this cop."

"Actually, you may hear from us again, Chief," Cecil said. "I'm guessing your wife will want us for 'lack-of-character' witnesses at your divorce hearing." Cecil laughed out loud as he and Vernon walked from the bedroom.

CHAPTER 47

She'd been stopped at so many police checkpoints in the final blocks leading to the Sea Breeze that by the time Cha Cha Miranda made her way through a gauntlet of primarily L.A. media people to the police command post, Captain Crenshaw already knew who she was and why she was there.

"You're texts are very informative, Miss Miranda." The captain said. "Just curious, were you texting while driving?"

"Never, sir," Cha Cha replied with a smirk.

The captain shook Cha Cha's "So you know who did it?"

"That's right, officer."

"Where have you been the last fifty years?"

"A prisoner to my own conscience," Cha Cha said, nervously stroking the lapel of her brown leather jacket.

Captain Crenshaw's blue-gray eyes performed the standard police "once over" of Cha Cha as she stood before him shifting her weight from one leg to the other. "Aren't you the one who had the affair – "

"My personal life has nothing to do with anything," Cha Cha said, her eyes flashing at the captain.

Captain Crenshaw swallowed heavily and then offered Cha Cha one of the portable chairs. "Why don't you start at the beginning?"

She sat down slowly. "I can't tell it here," Cha Cha said.

"Where are you going to tell it, at Rotary?" The captain sighed and rolled his eyes.

"You don't understand."

"You bet I don't.

"I want to go on television with Penny Sexton, poor girl, and tell everyone in town that the class of '62 isn't to blame. They have lived with the curse for a half century and tonight I will lift it from them."

The captain started to pace. "I could put you in jail for withholding evidence and interfering with police operations."

"Go ahead," Cha Cha said, bouncing to her feet. "Then the case will never be solved. Everyone in this town knows how bad your chief wants to close the books on this." Cha Cha picked up her purse from where she'd left it at the foot of the portable chair and placed the strap over her shoulder. "I figured Chief McWorter, Jr. would be here tonight."

"A little communications mix up."

"Please don't try to stop me," Cha Cha said as she stepped in the direction of the activity center.

"We had better be able to make an arrest once you've spilled the beans."

Cha Cha stopped and looked back at the captain. "Is that a threat?"

"Call it whatever you like, Ms. Miranda."

Entering the activity, center Cha Cha was surprised to find it so small. On TV it looked like any convention center. And there were so few people. It looked like hundreds on TV. It brought to mind the only time she'd ever been on TV. It was on Channel Three. She was invited as a guest chef on a Christmas special. It had to have been fifteen years ago. She remembered how fat she looked when she watched a video of the show.

What surprised Cha Cha even more was a changing of the guard. The woman she recognized from TV as Penny Sexton was giving over control of the scissors to a guy with gray hair and a flabby stomach. Cha Cha and everyone else took deep breaths as Penny and the guy switched hands on the scissors without the tips ever moving off Lance Vance's jugular. Penny then stepped behind the two men and accepted a glass of water from an ex-classmate. Her body appeared to shut down as she fell backwards and had to be propped up by several of the partygoers. Cha Cha wondered if Penny hadn't momentarily passed out.

To her surprise, the guy with the big gut talked directly to the camera. "I know I'm screwed for pinch-hitting for Penny in a hostage situation -- makes me as guilty as her -- but I figure I owe it to her." Every so often the guy stared down at his feet. "My conscience has kicked into overdrive. Hadn't been for me she might truly have been homecoming queen and...well, you can figure the rest." Reno dropped his head for a moment as if he was embarrassed by his confession. Meantime, Cha Cha noticed that Penny had remarkably regained her senses and was straining her neck in an effort to hear what Reno was saying.

"I know some of my classmates, if they can hear me, are figuring I've just had too much to drink tonight," Reno said with a laugh. "Hell, I'm just getting warmed up. I'm trying to be conscientious."

Cha Cha was worried he might not be as receptive as Penny to turning the microphone over to her.

"I figure it's about time I did something right in my life. As many of my former classmates have found out tonight, I've been kind of a career screw-up. I feel genuinely sad that Penny had to revert to breaking the law to chase away her own personal demons. As far as you cops listening are concerned, you too, Lance, it will all be over soon. Penny's just taking some quiet time." Reno stopped to look back at her. They smiled as their eyes met. "She's trying to figure if there's anything else she needs to say. I'm just holding down the fort until she gives me instructions."

Cha Cha realized she'd better act soon. She hurriedly searched the room for any sight of Zeke Clayton. Her revelation would have far greater impact if he were present. She didn't consider herself a vindictive person, but she'd already conceded that she was looking forward to watching him squirm. Finally, she spotted him next to the bar talking with an attractive blonde. "Some things never change," Cha Cha said to herself.

Confident the time was right Cha Cha brushed back her hair, adjusted a button on her jacket, took a deep breath and then stepped purposefully in Reno's direction. "I know who did it," she announced before even reaching Reno.

Reno's face lit up. "Would you repeat that?"

"I know who's responsible for the *skin flick* and that engineer's death."

"Wow! Hold the phone," Reno said, his eyebrows darting upward. "Do you have proof?"

"Yes. But, not about the death part."

"This had better not be a joke."

"It's not."

"In case those of you in the room couldn't hear..." Reno paused. "What's your name?"

"Cha Cha Miranda. Class of '62 Santa Barbara High School."

There were a couple of boos at the mention of the rival school and the sound of breaking glass. Zeke Clayton had dropped his drink on the floor.

"Cha Cha Miranda," Reno continued, "says she has proof of who is responsible for putting the *skin flick* on the air in '62."

Reno's announcement created a buzz in the activity center.

Zeke pushed at the broken glass with his foot and looked about as if he expected someone from the motel to arrive and complete the dirty work. At the same time, he motioned for Enrique, who'd cornered an attractive Latina caterer at the opposite end of the room. "Let's go," Zeke mouthed the words. Within seconds Enrique was at his side.

"What's up, boss?"

"Nothing good," Zeke said, his face spotted with perspiration. "We've got to get out of here, now. Follow me."

All eyes in the room was so focused on Cha Cha that Zeke and Enrique were able to slip out the side door unnoticed by everyone except the two cops who were stationed in their path just beyond the door. Following instructions to stop anyone exiting the building, the cops both pulled their nightsticks and ordered Zeke and Enrique to halt. Without breaking stride as he passed through the door, Zeke dipped his legs ever so slightly and launched his body at the cops, a move he'd perfected on the football practice field many years ago. He caught both of their soft bellies with his shoulders and knocked them ass over teakettle. Enrique contributed by trampling them. They sprinted down the block to the car. As they approached the Mercedes Zeke could hear Captain Crenshaw barking on his bullhorn.

"We have officers down!"

Zeke heard him say it over and over until the sound was finally drowned out by the squealing of the Mercedes' spinning tires.

Back in the relative calm of the activity center, Whitney Crawford stood on his tiptoes and waved his arms for attention. "Let me cross-examine this woman," he said no less than three times.

"Do you mind?" Reno asked Cha Cha. "He's a class member and a lawyer."

"I don't like the term cross-examine," Cha Cha said. "But I will submit to an interview if that's satisfactory."

"Okay, okay!" Whitney said, throwing his suit coat on as he advanced toward the standoff staging area.

Reno handed Whitney the microphone. "Make sure it's an interview, Whitney."

"Of course, of course," Whitney said. He was so charged by the sudden change of events he'd forgotten his tie. "Please excuse my informal nature," he said. "For the record, state your name and address," Whitney said, fondling his open collar."

"That sounds too much like courtroom procedure," Cha Cha said. "Why don't you let me tell my story and you can jump in with questions when the need arises?"

Whitney agreed. "It's not how I would do it, but proceed." He reluctantly extended the microphone to Cha Cha.

Cha Cha cleared her throat before beginning. "I'm a little nervous," she said.

Reno tried to help. "This is your ballgame, honey. Take all the time you need."

"Thanks," Cha Cha said, the semblance of a smile crossing her face for the first time. "Before I tell who's responsible, I must tell you why I've not come forward until tonight." Cha Cha exhaled deeply before continuing. "My father, God rest his soul, operated a gardening business at the time that this happened. He had clients all over Santa Barbara. When it got too big for him he sent for his brothers in Mexico, from a little town called *Ixtlahuacán*. There were three of them, each undocumented. They lived in our house for years. I was afraid the police would find out about them if I got involved in an investigation. I couldn't begin to think of placing my dad's business in jeopardy. Later, I was forced by a weak economy to bring family members from Mexico to help with my business." Cha Cha paused to allow the lump in her throat to subside. "Forgive me. This is difficult."

Whitney Crawford attempted to take the microphone from Cha Cha. "I just want to – "

"But, I'm not finished," Cha Cha said, pulling the microphone into her chest.

"I have some advice for you," Whitney said, the veins in his neck protruding. "Stop incriminating yourself. Every word you say is being recorded. Do you know what the penalty is in this state for employing illegals?"

"Of course, I do. I would never take the risk without knowing the possible consequences."

"As an attorney I must advise you to stop revealing information that can be used by police investigators to build a case against you."

"Remember, you agreed to let me talk."

"But not – "

"For Chrissakes, let her continue," Reno said.

"Thank you," Cha Cha said, tears forming in the corners of her eyes. "I'm motivated to come forward at this time because, like the gentlemen here," she acknowledged Reno, who was standing next to her and still holding the scissors to Lance Vance, "I need to do the right thing for once in my life. I've lived a selfish existence watching from a distance as your class of '62 suffered needlessly. I come here with a deep feeling of humility. This cleansing should have happened years ago."

Rather than take another stab at gaining control of the microphone, Whitney just leaned his head in toward it and spoke. "Can I ask you to produce an exhibit of evidence?"

"Back off, Whitney," someone in the crowd hollered.

Before Cha Cha could resume, Lance Vance spoke out. "Ah, I'm awfully sorry for the interruption, but I'm getting word in my ear from the studio, Ms. Miranda, that they'd like you to hold off naming names until after a commercial break. Is that possible?"

"No," Cha Cha, said, "this is not a drama. Real life doesn't pause for blowout car sales."

Those in the activity center clapped at Cha Cha's firm stand.

"It is time for me to produce the evidence. I've talked too long about my own suffering. I want to end the pain for those who are here tonight and the many other class members who chose not to attend this reunion."

Cha Cha opened her purse and pulled out the business card. "This card belongs to Doug Raichel who was the distribution manager for Virgin Valley Pictures. There is handwriting on the back." She flipped the business card over and read from it. *"Two on One* $14.95 is what it says. I'm sure you all know that was the name of the *skin flick* that played on Channel Three the night of June 19th, 1962."

"Where did you get the card?" Whitney Crawford said.

Cha Cha took a deep breath and closed her eyes just before she spoke. "I found it in the glove compartment of Zeke Clayton's car. We were dating at the time."

A hush fell over the activity center. All eyes instantly searched the room for the now departed Zeke Clayton.

"On the front of the card," Cha Cha continued, there is a phone number with an area code I don't recognize. I remember trying it but I kept getting some angry old man. Finally, I gave up."

Whitney interrupted. "Let me have the number before you turn that business card over to the authorities."

Cha Cha didn't acknowledge him. She paused to study the card. "There's also a brief note in a different style of handwriting. It says, 'Zeke. Hope this works for you."

"You bastard, Clayton," Reno Parris hollered while still administering the scissors to Lance.

"He's gone," someone hollered.

"He's gone?" Cha Cha said to herself. *"Carajo!"*

After sending half his stakeout forces code three in pursuit of Zeke, the captain himself appeared at the main entrance of the activity center. "Time to end this picnic," he growled, placing his hand on his revolver, which, for the moment, he kept in its holster.

"No, not yet," Penny yelled. "Not until you bring Zeke Clayton before this camera. The class of '62 and all of Santa Barbara want to hear from him."

"That's vigilante justice," the captain said. "I can't condone it."

"No one's asking anything of you, Captain. We're telling you to bring him to us. Right, people?"

A thunderous roar went up in the activity center.

"Better yet," Penny said, her energy seemingly restored to its pre-hostage taking level, "have Chief McWorter, Jr. deliver him. It's only appropriate." Penny smiled. "His daddy tried so hard to blame it on one of us."

There was another roar of approval from the partygoers.

His chest thrust forward, his chin held high Captain Crenshaw spun on his heels in a stylish about face and exited.

The partygoers began hugging one another. Reno offered a toast. "To the curse," he said. Wild screaming and hollering followed. "Let's have music," he said to *The Occasions*, who'd just finished packing up their equipment. "Make it champagne music! And somebody bring me a drink. I'm not going to jail sober."

Believing she'd proved her worth, Cha Cha exited the activity center without fanfare and reported to Captain Crenshaw's command post. She found him fuming at a lieutenant who was trying unsuccessfully to restore a picture to the police department's TV set.

"Would you like my evidence?" Cha Cha said as she approached the captain who was red in the face from rage.

"Lietutenant," the captain yapped at the young officer, who was sweating profusely. "Get away from the damn TV and take this woman's evidence and a statement." Captain Crenshaw placed his hand on Cha Cha's shoulder and steered her toward the lieutenant and then quickly picked up his two-way radio. "All units respond," he yelled into the mouthpiece, "does anybody copy me?" He waited a moment; when there was no response, he slammed the two-way to the asphalt. It bounced up so high he caught it. "Cheap shit is all that prick buys." He turned in Cha Cha's direction to find her watching his tantrum. "Yes, I am talking about the chief of police, if you must know."

"All I want to know," Cha Cha said, hands on hips, "is the way out of here, Captain."

Captain Crenshaw didn't respond. He just slammed the two-way to the ground one more time.

CHAPTER 48

Cecil could barely keep his eyes open. Had it not been from the static coming from the police radio in the Ford Taurus he might have been able to catch some much-needed shut-eye. "Why do you have to have that damn radio on, Vernon? Am I not good enough company while you're driving?"

"Cause I want to know what the cops are up to."

"Hey," Cecil said, abruptly sitting up in his seat. "Did you see that?"

"What?"

"The sign said Ojai."

"Oh hi to who?"

"Come on, Vernon. Haven't you ever heard of Ojai? They've got a great golf resort and spa there. Lots of Hollywood people stay there. I hear Michael Bolton's a regular."

"Who's he?"

"The singer."

"Where do you find this pertinent information?"

"Supermarket tabloids."

"You read that shit?"

"I mainly look at the pictures. But I manage to get most of their scoops."

"You use that term singer too loosely, Cecil. The last real singer was Tony Bennett."

"You're aging yourself, Vernon."

"Nah, singing is a lost art, Cecil. All there is now is a bunch of hoodlum rappers who say shit you or I wouldn't say to our worst enemy. And those names. Yesterday, I read a news story about Dog Barf EZ suing his record label because they were throwing all of their promotion money at his rival, F-Me Naked."

"Ah, you gotta change with the times, Vernon."

"Not me, Cecil."

"Back to my point, Vernon. We should turn around and head for that resort. I know we could unload the last of these *Power Strokes*. People who stay at that resort got money to burn."

"What are we going to do, have a tailgate party in the club parking lot? Maybe we can make it potluck. You know, invite Mr. Vacationing Corporate Executive to bring country style potato salad. We'll give everyone a fifteen percent discount who brings a dish."

"Now you're being hurtful."

"You just don't think things through, Cecil. Never have."

Almost as if it had heard enough bickering, the Ford's police radio started hissing and sputtering like someone was trying to make contact. Vernon searched for the volume button, but couldn't find it.

"C-Baker 12," a voice said. "Do you copy?"

Worried he might drive out of radio range at any second, Vernon quickly pulled the Ford to the curb.

"C-Baker 12, we have a situation here. Do you copy?"

Vernon and Cecil leaned in toward the radio so they wouldn't miss a word.

After a couple of minutes of nothing, the same voice came back on. "God fucking damn it, Chief, where in the hell are you? We've got a hostage situation going that requires your presence and I haven't heard from you since you left this fucking dump motel hours ago. Where in the fuck are you? Please respond immediately."

It appeared to Vernon that the key to the microphone at the other end was still open. He could hear two people talking, but it was feint.

"Cocksucker will show as soon as we capture the guy. Junior's always there when the fucking cameras roll. I'll bet he's got his dick stuck in some sexual assault victim's box as we speak. Oh, shit —"

"The chief doesn't appear to have a great deal of allegiance among the troops, Cecil."

"Maybe we should see that he gets fired, Vernon."

"That's the first good idea you've had since you suggested the Country Kitchen buffet back in Vegas."

"How do you suppose we transmit?"

"Just start pushing buttons, Vernon."

Vernon did until he hit the button for the siren. "Oh, shit!" Vernon shouted.

"Turn off the key," Cecil yelled.

Vernon did and the siren finally went off. Both of them craned their necks in every direction to see if it had attracted any attention. The Ford was stopped near the entrance to Ocean Colony, an upscale housing development not far from the freeway.

"Try it again," Cecil said.

This time, Vernon turned another volume button and keyed the mike at the same time. Bingo.

"C-Baker 12," came the same voice. "That you, finally?"

Vernon and Cecil took turns telling the voice at the other end exactly where they could find the Chief of Police and what he would be wearing.

The voice finally identified himself as Captain Crenshaw and wanted to know who in the hell he was talking to. But Vernon and Cecil both figured that even though they had pictures of the chief, they shouldn't press their luck. "Over and out," Vernon said, when he figured the captain had all the information he needed.

CHAPTER 49

The cab driver lied and said his passenger was a motel guest who was extremely ill from some sort of food poisoning. It allowed him to get through every one of the police checkpoints leading to the Sea Breeze where he dropped Janet Nyborg off not far from the command post. "It's on me," the cabbie said. "You've had a rough night considering your son and all."

"Thank you, Janet said, moving with a stiffness that suggested a minor arthritic condition. She nearly got swallowed up in the convergence of reporters.

"Are you somebody?" a woman with a microphone asked.

"Please state your name," yelled another woman reporter.

"You that Penny woman's sister?" a man without a tape recorder blurted. When Janet finally reached the command post she needed a breather.

"This is not a safe place for an elderly woman to be," Captain Crenshaw greeted her.

"Thank you officer, but I'm actually the same age as the people holding my son hostage."

"Your son?" the captain said. "Your son?" he repeated. Captain Crenshaw may not have had the smarts to grab the chief's position over Junior, but he knew an opportunity when he saw one. "Lance Vance is your son?"

"I'm hear to beg Penny to turn him loose. I can't stand by and watch him suffer any more." Janet worried she might be coming off as a little too traumatized.

"You've been watching TV?"

"Yes."

"Not a pretty sight."

"Especially not for a mother."

Sensing he might be able to put an end to the stand-off by playing the mother card, Captain Crenshaw escorted Janet in the direction of the activity center. He offered his arm as a steadying instrument.

At the entrance, Janet suddenly stopped and turned to face the captain. "There is more to my coming here than my son. You may want to pay close attention to what I have to say."

Captain Crenshaw's eyebrows lifted. Then came the reality of the situation. "Damn, I can't. My damn TV's out. Fucking piece of shit equipment. I swear the chief shops for this crap at Toys R Us."

Janet ignored the captain's response and walked far enough into the activity center for Lance to recognize her.

"What on earth are you doing here, Mother?"

Janet kept eyes trained on Penny. "I'm here to put an end to your holding my son hostage," she said, her voice cracking slightly.

"My God. You've just been upstaged," Lance said to Penny. Then he spoke directly into the microphone. "You folks back at the station, you might want to come out of this break early."

Janet made a gesture like she'd like help with her coat. Reno Parris accommodated her the best he could with only one free hand. In the process Reno felt the tension of the scissors lessen. Instantly someone yelled, "He's getting away." Reno snapped his head around only to find the scissors keeping thin air at bay as Lance, free of the IFB earpiece that kept him in contact with his producer, moved with a noticeable limp toward the front entrance.

"Stop!" Reno hollered. He sprinted after him, his heart pounding like he was racing to beat out an infielder grounder. Just as Lance reached the last step before the entryway, Reno launched himself like a base runner hurling himself at home plate. To his own surprise, he managed to clip Lance behind the knees with the full weight of his body. The two crashed to the linoleum floor; Reno on top. Within seconds, the scissors were back in place against Lance's neck. Breathing heavily, Reno was shocked by what he heard Lance whisper.

"Thanks man. I was counting on you catching me. It makes for dynamic TV."

Reno helped Lance back to his feet and the two of them returned to the familiar hostage anchor spot. "Thank you for not hurting him, Reno," Janet Nyborg said. She tried to move close enough to Lance to check his condition but Reno asked her to back off. "He's okay."

"Is that true, Lance?" Janet asked.

Lance nodded that it was.

"Do you remember me?" she said, turning to face Reno. "I'm Janet Nyborg."

Reno blushed. "My God, I do. Goleta Beach. The sophomore picnic."

"I'm impressed. The years haven't made off with your memory."

"Cops caught us?"

"They called my parents."

"Ditto."

Advised by Lance, who had hooked his IFB back into his ear, that Channel Three was returning live in ten seconds, Penny reclaimed the microphone and was introduced to Janet by Reno.

"I remember you," Penny said, with a wide smile. "You had to –"

"Those are painful memories, Penny. I'd rather not –"

"I'm so sorry," Penny said, her eyes shutting briefly.

"He's the reason I had to leave," Janet said, gesturing at Lance.

"I don't understand," Penny said.

Reno interrupted. "Penny, the man you have been holding hostage is Janet's son."

"So, it's one of those TV names," Penny said, her eyes widening as if to indicate she finally got it.

"Yes, one of those names."

Penny dropped the microphone to her side." Her eyes searched the ceiling. "I suppose you're here to talk me into surrendering and releasing your son?

"Eventually, I'd like to see him released, unharmed, but – "

Did the police bring you here?"

"I came on my own."

"Honest?"

264

Janet reached for the microphone. Penny instinctively recoiled.

"I have something I'd like to say."

"About what?"

"About why you're all here this evening."

Reno urged Penny to give up the microphone. "We owe her that much."

Lance was next to speak, his voice now raspy and weak. "Don't be fooled by the mother act. We're estranged."

"Foolishly so," Janet said. "What I have to say has nothing to do with being a mother and yet again it has everything to do with it."

"Well say it," Penny said with a sigh.

Janet looked down at her feet before she spoke and nervously grabbed at the back of her hair, momentarily forming a ponytail. When she finally spoke she struggled with the message. "I'm... confessing... to the... *skin flick...*" prank."

An eerie silence fell over the activity center.

Lance displayed a curious look.

Reno broke the silence. "No way! We just heard that Zeke Clayton was the one."

Janet shook her head no. "I was... behind... the... idea," Janet said, her voice cracking on each word.

A voice from the back of the room interrupted her. It belonged to Edgar Peoples. "This is some kind of crazy person, people. Truth be told, this room is full of whackos. I've had enough weirdness for one night." The sound of the side exit door opening and the clanking of his gold pieces around his neck indicated Edgar was good on his word.

"Why don't you let me interview her?" Lance said in between coughs. "It's what I'm trained to do."

"No dice," Reno said. "Mother or not you're still our hostage and that's what's keeping the cops at bay. I let you free to have a heart-to-heart with Mom and Blue is in this place faster than you can spell Miranda rights."

"Just be patient with me," Janet said, clearing her throat.

"Go ahead," said Penny.

Janet took a few seconds to allow the knot in her throat to subside. "When Mr. Nesbitt, the principal, told me I couldn't attend San Marcos because I was pregnant I felt betrayed. My parents didn't protest his decision, which made it even worse." Janet paused to request a glass of water. Bernie Wolfeson, the perennial science fair blue ribbon king, offered his.

"I was sent far away. At first I was depressed. I was lost and alone in a strange town. I had no friends and no one to confide in. My pregnancy was difficult. I had suffered from both high blood pressure and gestational diabetes. After Lance was born I became bitter. I wanted to strike back at those who'd rejected me: the principal, my parents, the boys who I'd had sex with who wouldn't come forward and be tested. I became filled with hate. I wanted to punish everyone who wasn't going through my misery. I did just that."

Whitney Crawford got out of his seat and approached Janet. "Cleans yourself, Ms. Nyborg .

Janet took Whitney's hand in hers. "Thank you."

"Please continue," he said.

"I put my plan to work as early as April of 1962. I wrote Edgar Peoples a long letter telling him about the birth of our son. Edgar was one of the boys, who, well, you get the picture. I enclosed a phony picture of a light-skinned black child and he bought it."

"Two days after I sent the letter, Edgar called me back. He was panicked. He told me his mother, a respected medical researcher, would disown him and take back his college money if she were to find out he'd fathered a child. Well, I had Edgar where I wanted him."

"No wonder he bolted this place," a guy from the back shouted.

Janet continued, unfazed by the interruption. "I told Edgar there was a way out for him if he'd do me a favor. I told him about my idea to run a *skin flick* on Channel Three and he agreed to carry it out for me in exchange for my not naming him the father. Why he would trust me and not take a paternity test is beyond me. I guess he was that scared."

"Fucking Edgar did it?" Reno said under his breath. "Mother fucker." This time it was loud enough for Janet to hear.

"I'm not surprised Edgar left" Janet said. "He and I damaged a lot of lives. I'm so sorry for Mr. Burdette. I never intended that to happen. I still haven't convinced myself that we didn't murder him by scaring him into a heart attack."

"What about Zeke Clayton?" Lance said, his reporter instincts overriding a deteriorating physical condition that now featured pale coloring, saliva at the corner of his mouth and a sagging posture.

"I watched her on TV before I left home to come here," Janet said, looking directly at her son for the first time. "She is very courageous, but her evidence only tells half the story, son."

"We've got the time," Lance said.

Janet nodded in agreement and continued. "Zeke Clayton and I were good friends when he got kicked out of school. In fact, well, I shouldn't embarrass myself any further. Let's just say I was a little loose as a teenager. I had no idea how to acquire a pornographic film that would be compatible with a TV station's equipment and Edgar was clueless to how he might put one on the air. I knew Zeke had been to some film school and was hoping, as early as 16, for a career in the movie business. I called and asked him to help. He was happy to, as he said, 'put the screws to anyone and everyone who had anything to do with San Marcos High School'. He ordered the film and talked Edgar through the mechanics. Ironically, Zeke had participated in a *students-at-work* day earlier that year and had spent time in Channel Three's master control learning how things operated."

Without warning Janet stopped her story and slowly sagged to her knees, burying her head in her chest as she reached the floor. She began to sob. "I'm so sorry," she said, and then repeated it. "Please forgive me." She rolled to her side and assumed the fetal position.

The sound of Captain Crenshaw's bullhorn broke the hush that had fallen over the activity center. "This is the police," he said.

"Now there's a revelation," Reno laughed.

It was quiet enough in the activity center that everyone could hear the captain key his bullhorn. "In ten seconds we are coming in…" The bullhorn began to sputter as if it had shorted. "We…are…testing, one …"

Reno surprised Penny by grabbing her arm and pulling her to him. It was all he could do to keep Lance Vance from bolting again. "Give me a second," he shouted at Lance, placing even greater pressure on the scissors. Reno's eyes blazed red with intensity. He turned to Penny and said, "I think Blue is ready to rush this place. You and I had better make tracks or we'll be picking up freeway trash for the rest of our lives."

Penny's confused eyes bounced like ping pong balls from Janet, to Lance, to the activity center entrance and back to Reno. "Let's try the back," she said.

"You know what they'll say about us leaving together," Reno said with a faint smile.

"They'll say 'poor Reno, he thinks he's finally going to get lucky'."

"Score one for the hostage lady." Reno then pulled the scissors from Lance's jugular. "Lets go!"

Penny turned to leave and then abruptly stopped. "Any new vote returns, Lance?"

Lance started to answer but then collapsed in a heap on the floor, his head coming to rest next to his mother's.

"Now I'll never know the final numbers," Penny said, looking into Reno's eyes.

"You'll be a number on a rap sheet if we don't get moving," Reno said, grabbing Penny by the hand and racing for the back exit as their classmates began chanting in unison: *"No more curse! No more curse! No more curse!"*

"Good luck guys," someone shouted as the door opened and closed.

A single cop, who was old enough to be on every security company's recruiting list, was stationed outside the rear door. He commanded the two to stop but Reno overwhelmed him, grabbing his nightstick and slamming it against his neck. The old cop dropped like a fading starlets boobs and Reno and Penny scrambled off, sprinting in the direction of a vacant lot that was surrounded by eucalyptus trees.

"Shit!" Reno said, his chest heaving for oxygen as he tried to stay even with a fleeing Penny. "That was better contact than I made in twelve years in the minors."

"It's going to get you at least that many years in the slammer if you don't pick up the pace."

"If I have to pick my poison I'll take capture over having my heart blow out of my chest."

"I always said you were a blowhard, Reno."

"You're getting sentimental, Penny."

As they emerged from the patch of eucalyptus, they spotted an alley ahead of them. If they could get to the ally without being detected they both figured they might actually have a chance to make good on their escape.

"Heading for home with a full load of mean," Reno yelled.

"And to think I almost let you do me."

"Missed one of the great thrills of your life."

"Yeah?"

"I do have a rain check policy."

They both laughed as they turned into the alley and slowed to a jog. Moments later they disappeared into the darkness of a path leading to an abandoned seminary.

CHAPTER 50

After escorting Sergeant Patterson from the emergency room at County and helping him into the passenger seat of his black and white, Dee Dee Wellborn got behind the wheel. "I've never ridden in the front of one of these," she said tapping his ribs with her open hand.

"Ooh!" Patterson said. "That's where I first hit; on my side."

"Sorry, I should have known better."

Sergeant Patterson had been treated for a severe contusion over his left eye. It took a dozen stitches to close the wound. He was advised by doctors not to drive home because of complaints of dizziness.

"So, where's home?" Dee Dee said.

"I don't want to go there," he said, as he winced from the pain caused by trying to adjust his seat. "Shoulda had them check my ribs. I think they're busted."

"You want me to turn back?"

"Nah. Just keep driving."

"Why don't you want to go home?"

"My old lady and me –"

"You're not wearing a ring."

"Never have."

"How long you married?"

"Three years."

"Newlyweds."

"Three years can be an eternity."

"So, why did you come back to the party after you got off duty?"

"To see you."

"Really?"

"Yeah. I liked your balls on that first hostage situation."

"I got news for you."

"I mean literally. Or, is it figuratively. I get the two of them mixed up. I might be dyslexic."

Without responding Dee Dee whipped the black and white across two lanes and squealed the tires as she negotiated a side street. Her judgment was off just enough that the black and white clipped a light pole with its front bumper.

"Christ almighty!" Patterson shouted.

"Just a little anxious," Dee Dee said, braking hard as she pulled perpendicular into a parallel parking spot.

"Does your seat tilt back?"

"Yes, but – "

"Just do it."

Wearing a puzzled look, Patterson groped the side of his seat for the power module. "What – ?"

"In case you haven't noticed, I'm impulsive. It's why I was such a lousy gambler."

"But – "

Dee Dee turned and reached across the gearbox console and tugged at the zipper of the Patterson's pants. "Are you serious,?" he said in high pitched voice.

"I am," Dee Dee smiled. "It's my specialty. You tell me when I'm done if I don't suck better than a moderately priced Hoover."

No sooner had Dee Dee applied her tongue to Patterson's baseball bat size unit than the black and white's radio came alive with dispatcher talk. "Damn," Dee Dee said pulling off Patterson's member. "I must have hit the power button with my elbow."

"C-Baker 10, 13 and 15, we have a suspect citing at Olive and Bath streets. A silver Mercedes coup with one Hispanic male driving and one white male in the passenger's seat."

"Shit!" Patterson said. "That's only a couple – "

"That's them," Dee Dee interrupted as the Mercedes screeched sideways past the parked black and white.

"Help me out of the car," Patterson said, straining to push the passenger door open.

"Oh, no, you're in no condition to drive, not to mention get involved in a chase." Having said that Dee Dee turned on the ignition, slammed the gearshift into drive and burned rubber for half-a-block. "This could be the most fun I've had all night, and that's saying something."

CHAPTER 51

"Where did that unit come from?" Enrique whined as the black and white driven by Dee Dee emerged from a side alley and locked onto to the Mercedes' tail. Enrique was doing 85mph and the newly arrived black and white was half a car length off his back bumper.

"It's a woman driving," Zeke said.

"You're kidding."

"You can't lose a woman cop, you're through driving for me."

Enrique pounded his foot against the accelerator. The Mercedes had enough thrust to snap their heads. "No wonder you wanted to make this picture, boss. You lived it. It's like fucking over someone and then putting it back in their face years later."

"There's an alley on your left. Take it!" Zeke said.

Enrique whipped the Mercedes into a sharp turn and car skidded wide enough to tap the passenger door against the side of an abandoned liquor store. "Sorry boss."

Zeke slammed his open hand against the dashboard. "It's all because Edgar Peoples chickened out, the little prick."

"Whose he and what do you mean?"

"The girl, yes the girl, who came up with the *skin flick* idea somehow got Edgar – he was the black guy at the reunion – to agree to pulling off the prank. I pretty much talked him through everything he'd have to do once he got into the TV station's control room. But, the night before it was to go down, he called and said he couldn't do it. He flat admitted to being too scared. He gave me some excuse about how his mother would pull his college funds if he were to get caught, but I could tell he was just scared. You know how a nigger's voice gets high when he's scared."

"Shit!" Enrique said as he masterfully swerved in time to avoid a big dog that had popped out from behind a Dumpster. "That was close, boss."

"Good move, Enrique."

"So you volunteered to take his place?"

"Seemed like a fun idea at the time."

"That took some gonads, boss."

"Like the girl, I had my issues with that school."

Enrique suddenly cranked the steering wheel hard left and guided the Mercedes out of the alley and onto a street that had been narrowed by construction barriers. "I don't see any major criminal offense in what you've" described to me."

"Well, I didn't figure on the guy dyeing."

"What guy?" Enrique's face spelled puzzled.

"Fuck," Zeke said, slamming a fist against the dashboard. "The engineer. He had a fucking heart attack right in front of me."

"You've got to be safe on statue of immitations, something like that. I read a lot about how murderers get off because of it."

"Statute of limitations," Zeke shouted. "Not for murder one. Not in California. I looked it up."

"Whatever boss."

"That top cop wants nothing more than to fry the killer and restore his dad's legacy."

"Then maybe you do got a problem, boss."

But there's something worse, Enrique."

Without warning, Enrique braked hard and hung a quick left onto State Street. "Shit!" he said, checking his rearview mirror. "I can't shake the bitch."

"The fire," Zeke said, appearing suddenly oblivious to the pursuing black and white.

"Fire?"

"I didn't want a paper trail so I paid a professional to torch the administration building at Valley Vista Pictures."

"Why?"

"I wanted my transaction record destroyed. The dumb fuck burned down the entire complex."

"Where'd you get that kind of money at what, age 18?"

"I was a football player at USC. They won the Rose Bowl the year I got there. Need you ask any more?"

Enrique managed to gain a car length or so on Dee Dee as he cornered again and roared east on Michelterena street. In the distance, maybe a quarter of a mile back, were two more police units. If only he could ditch the woman, he could get enough breathing room to make some evasive moves.

"Watch out!" Zeke hollered.

Enrique yanked the steering wheel hard to the left to avoid a pedestrian who'd appeared out of the darkness, thanks in part to a broken street light. The Mercedes went into a sideways skid, smacking hard up against the very light post. The pedestrian, a black man, who was grazed by the Mercedes' rear fender, was still on the ground when Enrique staggered toward him. The door on Zeke's side was jammed but he was too groggy to exit anyway.

"You okay, man?"

"No, fool!"

Just as the pedestrian made an attempt to rise, Dee Dee's black & white screeched to a halt no more than twenty feet from the Mercedes.

"Hands up," Sergeant Patterson said, struggling to get out of his car but pointing his revolver at Enrique. Then he turned to Dee Dee, who was checking out the Mercedes, and handed her a Derringer he'd taken from the inside of his boot. "Make sure that fuck doesn't move."

Once the sergeant had cuffed Enrique, he walked over to the pedestrian, who'd managed to get to one knee. He was brushing himself off when Patterson asked him what happened.

"Mutha fucker came out of nowhere," the pedestrian said. "Going way too fast."

"What are you doing in this neighborhood this time of night?"

"Made a liquor run. Had a bad night. My girlfriend left me."

"How come?"

"I'm not sure."

Convinced Zeke was too woozy to flee, Dee Dee walked over to Sergeant Patterson, whose large frame had momentarily screened her view of the pedestrian. "Who have we got here?" Dee Dee asked, trying to figure out what to do with the Derringer. "Mustafa?" she said, finally getting an unobstructed view of the pedestrian.

"Sweet thing?" Mustafa said.

"I'm not your sweet thing anymore."

"Sweet thing?" Patterson said, his eyebrows raised.

"The motel, the old farts…"

"Get on your feet, pal," the sergeant ordered Mustafa. "I think there's a public drunkeness charge with your name on it."

CHAPTER 52

Vernon had decided it was too dangerous for him to drive any farther without sleep so he pulled off the road into a highway rest area just south of Camarillo. He and Cecil spent a surprisingly restful night in the Ford and in the morning drove to a nearby Denny's for breakfast.

"I've been thinking," Cecil said while twirling his fork in a serving of scrambled eggs.

"You're going to turn yourself in," Vernon laughed.

"I'm going to turn myself into the studmeister. I used to be one."

"How's that?"

"I got one of those introductory offers online."

"For what?"

"It's a performance enhancer and it'll enlarge your penis."

"Jesus Christ, Cecil. This is not a suitable discussion over pancakes and sausages."

Cecil pulled a printout of an old email out of his jacket pocket. "Just listen to this. It's some Swedish product." He read from the paper: 'Up to seventy-four percent harder erections and from seven to twenty-six physical penile contractions', whatever that means."

"Why not seventy-five?"

"Who cares about one percent? Here's the capper. They guarantee your penis will grow one to three inches."

"What does it matter if you don't have someone to put it in, Cecil?"

"If I'm packing three more inches and I put on my swim shorts and drop into that water aerobics class back at the club, Mary Hirschbaum is gonna notice. I promise you, my friend."

"With your luck you'll hurt yourself getting into the pool, Cecil. Save your money."

Cecil ate the rest of his breakfast in silence, pausing occasionally to review the e-mail.

Vernon broke the silence with an idea of his own. "What do you think of maybe moving to Santa Barbara?"

"Mary Hirschbaum's one reason I'd be against it. I promised myself I'm going to get in her pants before she gets intercontinent."

"Incontinent."

"Whatever."

"Think about the leverage we have with that photo of the chief," Vernon said. "We could bribe him."

"Bribe him for what?"

"For the right to operate our club theft ring out of Santa Barbara without any police interference."

"That's good thinking, Vernon."

"You ought to try it some time."

"I told you I'm going for the introductory offer."

"Shit! You think only with your pecker."

CHAPTER 53

Rita Arenas was slow to take her cue coming out of a commercial break. She was caught punching numbers on a pocket calculator, apparently trying to figure how much she'd already made in overtime. If Tyler Tew hadn't cleared his throat to alert her, she might not have taken the cue until sunrise. In Rita's defense, it was 5:15 in the morning. That meant she and Tyler were into their sixth hour of *Assault at the Sea Breeze: A Reporter Held Hostage.* Tyler, with a fresh dousing of hairspray, appeared re-charged —he would later attribute it to his conditioning with the new Bowflex home gym he'd received for casually mentioning the product on several newscasts, while Rita was positively bleary-eye and slow of speech.

She was obviously influenced by her dramatically improving personal economics when she began an earlier segment by saying, "Updating tonight's time-and-a-half events ..."

The fact that D & L Motors had agreed to donate three slightly used Chevy Monza's for use as news cars weighed heavily on management's deciding on round-the-clock coverage.

Even though the hostage situation was over, Channel Three management was holding to the notion that there were plenty of peripheral stories to be milked: the police manhunt for Edgar Peoples, Sergeant Patterson's heroics, the whereabouts of Reno Parris and Penny Sexton, and how the D.A. might make a case of murder against Zeke Clayton..

Shortly before 9:00AM Rita and Tyler were informed by their news director they would finally be relieved from the anchor desk at noon.

"That's almost twelve-hundred dollars," Rita said, slapping her pocket calculator on the anchor desk during a commercial.

The mid-day anchor team of Liz Rollins and Walker Davidson was assigned to continue with the station's live coverage. But that all changed when one of the news department's associate producers received a phone call from the police department's Public Information Officer with word of a major announcement at 11:30AM.

Hearing this, Channel Three's news director ordered Rita and Tyler to continue as anchors to which Rita responded, "Can you say Maui in March?" The prospect of unexpected income seemed to energize her; that, and the arrival in the studio of the makeup artist, who said to the stage manager upon her arrival, "I'm here to freshen up "the bitch."

CHAPTER 54

At precisely 11:30AM, Vernon and Cecil entered Santa Barbara's lone Electric City store, which was ironically located only a stone's throw from the Sea Breeze motel. If it plugged in it could be purchased at Electric City. Cecil was looking for a toaster. "Can't go any longer without my bagels and cream cheese in the morning," he'd announced to Vernon. "This life on the road is hard."

When they passed by the TV section every single screen was showing City Manager Evan White talking to the media. Vernon grabbed Cecil by the arm.

"I'll bet this has something to do with..."

"Yep.

When they got close enough to a sale-priced Sony flatscreen, they could hear the city manager introduce Chief Franklin McWorter, Jr. who moved to the microphone.

The chief's face was drawn; there were bags under his eyes the size of airplane carry-ons. He shuffled some notes on the podium that was decorated with a police department shield. His voice was quiet; his manner subdued. "It's with great regret that I offer my resignation as your police chief," he said, halting several times to catch his breath. "It's especially difficult now that we appear to have closure in the *skin flick* caper, which blemished my father's legacy for far too long." Junior paused to drink from the water glass on the podium. "I'm leaving the department after twenty-six years of service for personal reasons. The job of chief is extremely high profile and is very time consuming. It can easily impact one's personal priorities. I apologize to my wife and family for compromising my commitment to your service."

Cecil elbowed Vernon who was standing next to him. "Our Kodak moment just blew up in our faces."

"Sure did. So much for leverage on a disgraced police chief."

Cecil scratched his head. "I guess informing the second in command, what's his name?"

"Crenshaw."

"Wasn't such a good idea."

"Kinda like buying patio furniture before a tsunami."

Just then, a pasty skinned Electric City salesman, who looked unbelievably uncomfortable in his blue blazer and tie, interrupted their conversation. "Are you gentleman looking to buy or are you just looking because it's convenient and without charge?" he said, jabbing at the heavily jelled spikes in his hair. "You be surprised how many old guys like you come in here every day to watch *Dr. Phil*."

"Actually, we're looking for a steal," Cecil said, grinning at Vernon.

"I've got just the TV for you," the salesman said, pointing to a silver big screen TV in the corner of the entertainment department.

"Apparently you're not very civic minded," Vernon said to the salesman.

"How's that?"

"Your police chief is resigning and you don't appear to be the least bit interested."

The salesman winced. "That scumbag. I could care less. He's just getting what he deserves."

"How so?"

"It's all over the radio, this morning. He got caught porking some babe half his age in the middle of that hostage situation last night. Ron & Don on 1530 were slamming the guy pretty bad for neglecting his job and f-ing around on his wife. I guess somebody had pictures."

"" Imagine?" Vernon said. "Who would do something like that to a dedicated public servant?"

"Don't know, but I'd like to shake their hand," the salesman said with a grin.

Cecil extended his hand, and said, "Nice to meet you young man."

The salesman was left without a reply as the two would-have been customers exited the store.

CHAPTER 55

Edgar Peoples' brief flight from the law ended when he was stopped by a CHP officer in San Jose for driving a vehicle with expired tags. Edgar had hotwired a Pontiac Firebird a couple of blocks from the Sea Breeze and was believed headed for the Canadian border; at least that's what investigators from the Santa Barbara Police Department deduced after learning he'd placed a French dictionary in the glove compartment of the Firebird.

Edgar was extremely cooperative with arresting officers. He went to great lengths to substantiate Janet Nyborg's account of the evening of June 19th, 1962.

Zeke Clayton, who suffered a slight concussion and a broken arm in the crash of the Mercedes, hired L.A.'s top criminal defense lawyer to represent him after he was presented with statements Edgar Peoples made to investigators. Edgar sang like a carnival parrot. He even confessed that he'd never informed Janet Nyborg of the last minute switch with Zeke.

Two days later, *The Hollywood Reporter* published a report that the newly appointed police chief of Reseda was reopening the dormant investigation of the 1962 Virgin Valley Pictures fire. The front page story told of how the new chief planned to interview an eighty-five-year old San Quentin inmate who was doing a life sentence for murder, but who'd also had a history of arson in the San Fernando Valley in the early 60s. The new chief stated he understood that the statute of limitations do apply to arson but that he just wanted the long standing case resolved.

Variety followed up with a guest column by Media Vista Productions CEO Andrew Schuller, who dismissed the concept of due process and called for Clayton to step down immediately as head of Clayton Pictures. "Using a film, regardless of its nature and content, as an instrument in a destructive prank is blasphemous when orchestrated by someone within the film industry itself," Schuller opined. "It doesn't matter if he was just a high school kid at the time. "Zeke Clayton has given everyone who ever worked in the film industry a black eye."

✲ ✲ ✲

In a hastily called post *skin flick* caper investigation news briefing designed more to coronate himself than to produce relevant information, newly appointed Santa Barbara police chief Edwin Crenshaw applauded the efforts of Whitney Crawford in helping to crack the case. "He was dogged in pursuit of the truth," the chief gushed.

A day after Chief Crenshaw's public acknowledgement, Whitney took out a full-page ad in the Santa Barbara News Press and saluted himself. It read:

"I get results, even if it takes fifty years."
Whitney A. Crawford, Esq.

The same day the ad appeared, Whitney asked Wendy Overton to the Chamber of Commerce's annual Black and White Ball at the Four Seasons Biltmore. She accepted saying, "I'm sure there are a thousand other women you could have invited."

✳ ✳ ✳

Cha Cha Miranda was so relieved at having the burden of proof lifted from her shoulders that she made a special offer to any and all members of the San Marcos High class of '62. She announced a free banquet at Casa de Cha Cha; promising an open bar and a headline entertainer as well. "As a lifelong resident of Santa Barbara," she was quoted in the News Press, "I feel I have an obligation to help right the wrong that's been done to the class of '62."

The night of the banquet Carl Richter made a surprise appearance and cornered Cha Cha shortly after she had taken a break from receiving guests. Tanned and dressed comfortably in Tommy Bahama shirt and slacks, Carl informed Cha Cha that he had filed for divorce from Stella that morning. He asked Cha Cha for a second chance. She told him, "Fat chance," and walked away knowing full well she was lying to herself.

Less than 48 hours after the hostage drama, *Dee Dee Wellborn* told close friends she was getting married for a fourth time. She said Lieutenant Irv Patterson – he received an immediate promotion for his beyond-the-call-of-duty heroics in driving the squad car that chased down and led to the arrest of Zeke Clayton -- was the kind of man who would keep her from ever breaking the law again. "And he wants to please me," is how she signed off on any and all correspondence regarding her announcement. She neglected to tell anyone that she'd fudged a little in her account of the car chase.

After careful consideration, Scott Clayton, who was looking at a Three Strikes infraction until Enrique finally confessed to planting the cocaine on him, and Linda Dalby decided writing a book about the class of '62 was, in fact, an excellent idea. Scott was angry with himself for not thinking of it earlier. Linda said she would participate only if Scott would promise to pursue the project as a film.

"Nothing would give me greater satisfaction than to steal your dad's idea and make millions from it," Linda said with a grin.

"Not even another try at marriage?" Scott said, while the two were walking the beach in Hope Ranch.

"Is that a proposal, Scott?"

"If it's not, I've wasted a lot of time in rehearsal."

✡ ✡ ✡

Anthony Castello was smiling for the first time in a week, having just taken a call from the owner of the Sea Breeze motel. The owner told him that he had nominated Anthony for "Manager of the Year" at the just concluded Central Coast Hoteliers annual meeting. He admitted to nominating himself for "Owner of the Year."

"Your marketing skills are unequalled," the owner said to him. "For you to take the San Marcos lass reunion, a potential disaster if there ever was one, and turn it into a marketing home run deserves recognition. Hell, they'll probably declare the Sea Breeze a historic landmark one day."

Gracious to a fault, Anthony nonetheless decided to ask his boss for a raise rather than a nomination.

His boss responded by saying, "When did you become such a capitalist?"

"How is it you say? When opportunity knocks, you need to say, hold on; I be there in a second."

✡ ✡ ✡

A week had passed since Penny Sexton had taken Lance Vance hostage and had received bullpen help from Reno Parris. Santa Barbara police reported no progress in their attempts to apprehend the pair. Chief Crenshaw announced a fifty thousand dollar reward for their capture.

"We have reason to believe they are together and may have fled to Mexico," the chief said in an exclusive interview with Channel Three's Lance Vance. "We believe Mr. Parris has one, if not two, ex-wives living in the state of Nayarit. We're working closely with Mexican authorities, but so far there are no leads. My department will continue vigorous pursuit of these two fugitives from justice.

EPILOGUE

Visitors to the Pacifico Café, a small Mexican restaurant that backs up to the Pacific Ocean in the small town of Bucerias, located about thirty-minutes north of Puerto Vallarta, couldn't help noticing the gringo couple at the table nearest the back exit. The man was talking on a cell phone, quite loudly. Even though most in the café were Mexican tourists and didn't speak English, they could tell by the bulging veins in the neck of big gringo with the big *panzon* hanging over his belt was steamed.

"I don't care what my contract says, if you can't find me you can't sue me. Christ, Herman, I just called to give you a heads up that my radio career is done and you go Legal Zoom on me." There was a pause at Reno's end. It was long enough for Penny to mouth the words, "Tell him to tell Pearl that it's over between you two."

Reno smiled at the mention of Pearl and then returned his undivided attention to the phone call that he'd initiated. "What don't you understand about 'fugitive from justice', Herman? You think I'm going to saunter into work next week, punch my time card, open my mike and ask where Serena Williams' booty belongs in relation to the great bootys of all time like nothing ever happened? Christ, the Feds would have the station surrounded like we were Branch Davidians. Fuck, Herman, there are more important things in life. Besides, this call is costing me an arm and a leg." Reno flicked his cell phone shut.

Penny Sexton smiled across the table at Reno and nipped at the edge of a tortilla chip.

Reno was pleasantly surprised at how refreshed Penny looked less than forty-eight hours after her hostage ordeal. Her cheeks were rosy again, her eyes were back to reflecting mischief as he'd always remembered them and she was laughing; something he hadn't seen her do since early on the night of June 19th.

"You still have that uncanny knack for pissing off the world, Reno. It's remarkable that you've stayed so consistent over the years."

Reno tugged on his Margarita. "The best thing I've ever had in my mouth."

"Give me a chance at that," Penny grinned.

"Why didn't you say that fifty years ago?"

"Because you weren't protected. I was determined not to conceive at the f-ing drive-in. Imagine if I'd had to have told a daughter that it happened when Carry Grant and Doris Day were...you know, in *That Touch of Mink*."

"I don't think Doris Day ever bonked anyone."

"Well, it was implied."

Reno laughed and then changed the subject. "Last night, we talked about this being the chance of a lifetime, didn't we? Actually, I think you called it a chance at a new life." Or, did the tequila mess with my mind?"

"We did and I did."

Reno finished his Margarita and poked at a chicken enchilada with his fork. "Are we really on the same page today? Are we really up to changing our I.D.s and finding work selling timeshares until mid-day? Are we up really up to helping build houses for the poor in our spare time?"

"This time I'm going to be a blonde."

"I guess that means yes."

"My one virtue is that I'm good on my word," Penny said taking a bite out of a tasty shrimp. "First thing we're going to do is pick up a tool set at one those roadside flea markets. We can't help build houses without a hammer and nails, buddy."

"You feel good about this idea, don't you, Penny?"

"The thought of devoting my previously screwed up life to others absolutely invigorates me. I've never really had a purpose before. And you? It was, after all, your idea."

Reno ordered another Margarita. "A dozen before lunch is my limit," he said, his brown eyes dancing. "I discovered something the night of the reunion, Penny."

"Ooh, this sounds deep. I suppose you're going to tell me that you always liked me best."

"I realized that not only was I still attracted to you but that I had a whole new respect for you."

"All because I wouldn't put out."

Reno downed his Margarita and then stood and offered Penny his hand with the promise of a long walk on the beach. As they started down the steps to the beach, a per-spiring Mexican man who was sitting romantically close to his dark haired woman pointed at Reno first, then Penny. "*Usted* Carry Grant *y usted* Doris Day." The restaurant balcony suddenly rocked with laughter followed by warm applause.

Along the beach Reno looked for shells as he wandered aimlessly. "Let me tell you about what I discovered the other night. I'm being serious for a change."

"What was it?" Penny said, momentarily darting off line to hurdle late breaking whitewater.

"My thinking has changed. I don't think there ever was a curse.

"What about Edna Pendleton Wright's vendetta? I know first hand how much power that woman packed in both her public and private life."

"Oh, I believe she spent most of her adult years trying to screw over class members. I'll never dispute that fact."

"Your argument is taking on water, Reno."

"Hear me out, Penny."

"I'm all ears."

"Every person at that reunion – at least the ones I talked to – made bad decisions. That's why so many of us have had screwed up lives. Edna whatshername didn't make Vaughn Berglund do acid, Vaughn chose to. She didn't make Dee Dee Wellborn into an embezzler. Dee Dee chose to steal. Wayne Preston wasn't doomed to fulfill the prophecy of being the least likely to succeed, he chose to exist to surf. The old lady didn't set my baseball career in a tailspin by getting me demoted, I chose a lifestyle that required adult supervision 24/7 and as a result I didn't put in the work that it took to hit the curveball."

Penny stopped at a rope that tied a small swimmer's dock to a large beam on shore. "You're theory is sound until it comes to me."

"Explain."

"Edna Wright did put me through hell. When she found out I was having an affair with the judge she hired a stalker who tracked me everywhere. His mission was to make my life miserable by destroying my property and possessions. He punctured the tires on my Nissan twenty-some times, shot out windows in my apartment when I wasn't home, had my cat hanged from an oak tree at the entrance to my apartment complex. He painted the word adulteress on my garage door. Once he burned a cross in the tiny front yard. I'd go to the police. They'd take my report and that would be the end of it. I gave them detailed descriptions of the guy, but they never could nail him." Penny paused for a breath when she realized the recall of those events was causing her face to feel hot.

"But you chose to sleep with the judge, didn't you?"

"Well..."

"A bad choice."

"Wait!" Penny said, placing her face up in Reno's. "You screwed me out of being nominated for homecoming queen. That wasn't about a bad choice."

"You chose a rubber."

"You bastard," Penny said, swallowing her anger and at the same time bursting into a smile as wide as the shoreline.

They walked another half mile in silence before Penny spoke again. "This idea of yours that we both commit to making a difference in the world; you're sure it's the right choice?"

"It's our only choice if we want to make thing right with ourselves."

Penny suddenly stopped as more whitewater lapped at her ankles. She turned and smiled at Reno and without warning leaped into his chest, placed her arms around his neck and brought her lips to his, once, twice, a half-a-dozen times. "I'm happy to announce there is no longer a need for a condom."

"*Yes!*" Reno shouted loud enough to be heard by all the ships at sea, not to mention a once perceived demon or two.

Class of '62

By

Pete Liebengood